MW01222148

A BLAKE HARTE MYSTERY

CONFESSIONAL

ROBERT INNES

A BLAKE HARTE
MYSTERY
BOOK 2

OTHER BLAKE HARTE BOOKS

Untouchable
Confessional

CHAPTER

ONE

The village of Harmschapel was quiet as it slowly became enveloped in the orange glow of the evening's sunset. Flocks of birds that had been tirelessly singing all throughout the day slowly became silenced, leaving nothing other than the odd starling competing from opposite sides of the surrounding fields.

The gentle sound of two feet tapping carelessly against a stone wall did nothing to break the stillness. The panoramic view from this wall had always been Harrison's favourite part of the village. He was sat atop it, with his legs dangling over the side. He had sat on this wall since he was a child, sometimes when his parents had brought him into the village to do their shopping, or at other times when he had been a little bit older and had been allowed to come here on his own. As he had gotten taller over the years, his feet had slowly gotten closer to the ground, but even today, on his twenty-third birthday, they weren't quite there. Deep down he hoped they never would reach and that he would always be able to have his feet just hanging in the air.

Harrison closed his eyes so that the sounds around him grew just that little bit louder. His muscles began to relax, and the intrusive thoughts in his mind started to slowly disintegrate. It had been a long day.

Harrison hadn't told anybody about his birthday as he had not wanted the reminder that he was in the village, on his own, with no real family or friends around him, on his one special day of the year. And while he didn't feel the need for anybody to know about it, the one thing he didn't want to feel today was sad and lonely, so he was content to just settle for general apathy.

Unfortunately, one thing sitting on this wall had always done was clarify his feelings. The wall had helped him through quite a few of the toughest times of his life. When he was ten and had smashed his mum's favourite plate while playing in the kitchen, he had ran out of the house and come here to help decide how to own up to it. When he was sixteen, he had stared out over the same fields in exactly the same place and come to terms with his sexuality, and then a week or so later had debated how he was going to tell his parents. What he couldn't have known then was that a few years later, he would be sat here again with the side of his stomach throbbing angrily as a result of his then boyfriend, Daniel, hitting him for no good reason and trying to work out why.

Sitting here helped things make sense. But right now, for the first time he could feel himself fighting that familiar feeling of clarity as he came to the somewhat miserable conclusion that he did, in fact, feel incredibly sad and lonely. The sun was setting on his twenty-third birthday, and for the first time in his life, nobody had said '*Happy Birthday*' to him.

This was the first birthday that Harrison had spent on his own. A year ago today, neither of his parents had been in prison because at that time, they hadn't worked together to murder his ex-boyfriend. That had all changed six months ago. And while Harrison had finally started to adjust to his new life, living alone with his goat, Betty, who he had kept since childhood, today was tough.

The thought of Betty suddenly reminded him that he needed to feed her so he swung his legs up and over the wall, and began his walk home. In a strange way, he almost felt annoyed at the wall for letting him down. It hadn't helped him with anything in particular other than forcing him to embrace feelings that he had been trying to keep hidden all day. Doing an all day shift at the shop he now worked at had helped somewhat, but now that was over, he was left with little to distract him.

It wasn't long before Harrison found himself strolling past the police station, which meant he was only a few minutes away from his cottage. It was quiet, much like the rest of the village around him. The evening was drawing in quickly now, and the lights from the windows were orange and glowing gently. Harrison stopped and watched the building, as the wild and completely foolish thought of him strolling in and asking if DS Blake Harte was on duty went through his head. Quite what he would do if the answer to that question were yes, Harrison had no idea.

"Don't be stupid," he said to himself. He continued walking past the station and as he was silently thanking sense for prevailing, he heard a voice he instantly recognised.

"Harrison?"

Harrison froze. It was Blake. Harrison frantically wondered how his hair was looking, felt grateful for the fact that he was wearing a coat that covered up his work uniform, took a deep breath, and turned around, with a grin.

"Oh, hi Blake!"

Blake was standing at the door to the police station, ecig in his hand. He wandered across to Harrison, with a genuine smile on his face, one that Harrison quickly realised was less manic than his own.

"How have you been?" Blake asked. "I haven't seen you about in a while. Well, not since…"

His voice trailed off. Harrison grimaced and shrugged.

"I'm doing OK."

"I'm sorry about that night at the pub," Blake said. He sucked on his ecig, which then began flashing intermittently. "Bugger. Out of battery."

"Don't worry about it," Harrison replied. "Was your friend alright the next day?"

Blake grinned as he put the ecig back into his pocket. "No, she was ridiculously unwell. Still, the amount of cider she drank does that to a person. I didn't have a single shred of sympathy for her."

Harrison laughed, then put his hands deep into his pocket, desperately thinking of something else to say. His brain had gone completely blank. There was a few seconds silence, which felt like an age.

"Well, I best get back," Blake said. "You take care."

He turned to walk back into the station. From out of nowhere, Harrison suddenly said, "It's my birthday today."

Blake turned round, his eyebrows raised. "Yeah? Well, Happy Birthday! Have you got much planned?"

The last thing Harrison wanted Blake to know was the truth about his lack of celebration for the day.

"Oh, you know," he shrugged. "The usual."

"Well." Blake smiled. "I really hope you enjoy it. Don't do anything I wouldn't do."

Fat chance, Harrison thought to himself bitterly. "I won't. Promise," he said instead.

Harrison turned and walked off down the street towards his house, unable to stop himself smiling happily. If only one person was going to wish him a Happy Birthday today, he couldn't have been happier that it was Blake.

CHAPTER

TWO

Filled with sympathy, Blake watched as Harrison wandered off down the street. Throughout his time in the job, there had been few people he had dealt with who had had to go through such huge emotional upheaval as Harrison Baxter. He thought back to a couple of months ago and the night he had seen Harrison in The Dog's Tail. Blake's best friend, Sally-Ann, a sergeant from his old position before he had moved to Harmschapel, had been visiting, and as soon as she had clapped eyes on Harrison, Sally had tried to set the two of them up. Although at first Blake hadn't considered Harrison in any other way than a segment of the case he had been working on. With all of that over he had realised that Harrison was a really lovely person – certainly a million miles away from Blake's ex, Nathan, who he had discovered cheating on him with a woman.

But while Harrison and Blake had been getting to know each other, and the smallest possibility for a mutual attraction had begun, Sally had quickly brought an end to the proceedings. The last cider she had downed had been one too many and she had projectile vomited all over the bar before she could get herself to somewhere more discreet. Blake had been forced to say goodnight to Harrison only to take Sally home, where she had promptly passed out on his living room floor, not rising again till the next morning.

Ever since that night, Blake had found himself wondering what *could* have happened between him and Harrison but he had not had the opportunity to find out.

Blake walked back towards the station entrance cursing himself for not bringing his ecig charger to work. The unsatisfying performance from his ecig had left the need for nicotine clawing at him. He had been trying desperately to quit smoking over the past year, with limited success, often finding himself standing in a shop asking for a pack of his usual tobacco.

As he re-entered the meeting room, everyone was in exactly the same position as when he had left them. PC Billy Mattison was sat opposite PC Mini Patil, both tapping idly at their computers.

"So, go on Sir," Mattison said once Blake had settled down again. "Did you download it?"

Blake sighed. "Yes, Matti. I downloaded it."

"And?"

"And I don't think it's for me.

"Oh, come on, Sir!" Patil grinned. "You don't know unless you try."

Blake rolled his eyes and pulled his mobile out of his pocket, loading up the dating app that the two of them had suggested to him when he had made the, he now realised incredibly foolish move, of mentioning that he was a bit bored of being single to them.

Mattison stood up and came behind Blake, looking at his phone as the app cheerfully sprung into life as if it was convinced it was the answer to all of Blake's problems. "There's got to be somebody here you fancy, Sir. What about this guy?"

Blake stared at the profile of the man who had appeared on his phone. Admittedly, he was very good looking and a quick glance over his details revealed a few similar interests to Blake.

"Yeah, alright. He's nice."

"So, swipe right," Patil said.

Blake flicked his thumb to the right on the screen.

"Okay, now what?"

"Well, if it doesn't say you've matched with him, Sir, then he either hasn't come across your profile yet, or…"

He glanced at Patil who rolled her eyes. "Or, Sir, it means there's plenty more fish in the sea."

Blake frowned and stared at his phone as a picture of another man appeared. He looked to be in his late fifties and clearly was hoping for his incredible personality to shine through rather than relying on his profile picture. Blake grimaced at '*Teddy Bear*' and hastily flicked left on his screen.

As much as it made him cringe that he was getting dating advice from his two youngest officers, Blake had to admit that his love life of late had been completely non-existent. Clearly, the life of a Detective Sergeant wasn't seen as attractive as it had been before he had moved to Harmschapel.

He continued on his swiping mission, flicking left and right on his phone, not once coming across the words '*It's a match!*' that Mattison had promised him he saw on his phone all the time. But then, a face appeared that stopped Blake in his tracks. Harrison Baxter smiled up at him from his phone screen, his blonde hair styled modestly and yet probably unintentionally perfectly. His gentle features gave Blake a warm feeling in the pit of his stomach. His thumb hovered over Harrison's face. He knew which way he wanted to swipe, but he sincerely doubted that his phone would give him the response he wanted. Blake wasn't even sure he knew what the response he wanted was.

Instead he pressed the button on the side of his phone and put it back in his pocket, shaking his head, The whole dating app thing was ridiculous to him anyway – if you wanted to meet somebody, what was wrong with going to a pub or a bar and actually coming across somebody face to face? Blake didn't consider himself to be much of a fantasist but it seemed more romantic when asked where he had met the love of his life, to reply that fate had brought them together over a crowded dance floor rather than they had both happened to be online at the same time.

"See anybody you like, Sir?" Patil asked him over her computer screen.

"No, not really," Blake lied. "Maybe I'm just the best looking gay man in Harmschapel. Who knows?"

Patil laughed. "Maybe you are, Sir."

At that moment, the doors to the meeting room flung open and Sergeant Michael Gardiner stormed in.

Blake glanced up at him as Gardiner kicked his chair out from underneath his desk and threw himself down on it.

"Evening, Michael." Blake said cheerfully.

Gardiner glared at Blake. "Someone at the front desk for you."

"Me? Who is it?"

"Well," Gardiner replied brusquely. "Not necessarily just for you, one of you two can go. I don't care. I've dealt with her the past two times she's been in, and frankly, I have better things to be getting on with."

A groan rippled its way through the office.

"Oh, don't make go and talk to her, please, Sir," pleaded Mattison, sinking down into his chair. "She hates me. She's hit me with her umbrella before. That's assault!"

"Matti, she's eighty-one. She couldn't assault you if she tried." Blake grinned.

"She's surprisingly fast for her age," Patil said, looking just as reluctant to go anywhere. "Remember when those lads sprayed graffiti over her back fence? She actually properly ran after them. She's terrifying."

Blake rolled his eyes. "Alright, alright, I'll go. But don't think I'm not making a note of this sudden willingness to throw your boss to the lions."

He stood up, waggling his pen at Mattison who looked positively relieved.

When Blake arrived at the reception desk, he found Sergeant Mandy Darnwood looking furiously at the elderly woman standing in front of her. The second she saw Blake, Darnwood's expression changed drastically.

"Okay, there you go Mrs Atkins. DS Harte will

deal with your complaint."

She pressed the notepad in which she had been scribbling into Blake's chest, grabbed her cigarettes from underneath the desk, and quickly left the office.

Blake watched her make her frantic escape out the back door with his eyebrows raised, and then turned to the angry looking woman behind the desk. She was glaring at Blake expectantly, her wrinkled mouth was screwed up tightly. She narrowed her eyes at him, which made her entire face look not dissimilar to an old walnut.

"Well?" Imelda Atkins snapped. "What are you going to do about the noise?"

"What noise?" Blake asked, eyeing the umbrella that she had firmly gripped in her hand.

"The noise coming from across the road from my house!" Imelda exclaimed, looking at Blake as if she thought he was the most stupid man on earth. "It's those bloody college students! Booming music out at all hours of the day – not that I'd call it music, just noise! I'm fed up with it!"

Blake's eyes glazed over as Imelda continued ranting at him.

"And you know *full well* that this isn't the first time I've complained about this. As a matter of fact, this is the *third* time I've either had to come in or ring. And I've had *enough*! I want these people arrested! I know my rights as a citizen."

Blake sighed. "Mrs Atkins, I can't arrest a group of teenagers for playing loud music. Especially not at six o'clock in the evening."

"Well, what are you going to do?" snapped Imelda. "What are you for if it's not to keep the public safe and happy?"

"Right," Blake said as politely as he could muster. "I am due to finish very soon. I will go across to the house on my way home and tell them that they need to not play their music at an unreasonable volume."

"You mean order them —"

"Yes, yes," Blake replied, a little sharper than he had intended. "I will order them to keep the noise down. Alright?"

Imelda's lips somehow thinned even further. "Hmm. Well, just see to it that you do." She picked up her handbag from the reception desk and thrust it up her shoulder. "I'm off to evensong at the church now. I trust when I get home, it will be to peace and quiet?"

"Yes, Mrs Atkins." Blake grimaced. "I promise you that by tonight you won't be hearing a thing."

"Good." Imelda sniffed. She sauntered out of the station, putting her umbrella back into her handbag. Blake briefly wondered whether she had got it out purely as an intimidation technique.

"Is she gone?"

Darnwood was stood in the doorway to the office, the scent of cigarette smoke clinging to her. The smell triggered Blake's nicotine cravings again.

"Yes. Give me a cigarette."

Darnwood narrowed her eyes. "Aren't you supposed to have packed them in?"

"Yes. Give me a cigarette."

Darnwood shook her head. "You want to try chewing gum. My fella swears by them. It gives your mouth something to do. You'll thank me when the craving goes away."

Blake grimaced and rolled his eyes, walking out of the reception office and back into the meeting room.

Mattison looked up from his computer screen as he stormed through the door.

"What did she want?"

Blake picked his jacket up off his chair and flung it over his shoulder grumpily. "She wanted me to lock up a group of college students for playing music too loudly. Now, I'm going home, unless there's any more pensioners you lot are too scared to face?"

Mattison and Patil glanced at each other, amused. "No, Sir," said Mattison. "See you in the morning."

"She had her umbrella with her then?" Gardiner asked wryly, not looking up from his computer screen.

Blake's nicotine cravings scratched at him again as he grunted in reply and left them to it. It amazed him how quickly the hankering for a cigarette could diminish his mood. If he didn't get one soon, then the college kids he now had to visit on his way home probably would find themselves being locked up before the night was over.

Admittedly, the music was quite loud. Blake was leaning against a wall opposite the house, listening to the heavy drum and bass exuding from it. He had picked up a ten pack of cigarettes from a shop on the outskirts of the village and was now smoking one, regretting every inhalation. He finished it and flicked it into the nearest drain, conceding he had been a trifle optimistic when he had reduced the nicotine in his ecig to zero milligrams, and walked purposefully towards the house, knocking sharply on the door.

After a moment or two, the door opened and Daryl Stuarts, a tall, lanky teenage boy was stood in front of him, clutching a can of beer in each hand.

"Hello, Daryl," Blake said, eying the beer and discreetly sniffing the air to check that there wasn't anything more interesting than beer being enjoyed at the party.

Daryl's face dropped as he realised who Blake was. "Alright?"

"I didn't realise you were old enough to be drinking. My invite to your eighteenth must have got lost in the post. Unless it hasn't happened yet?"

Daryl futilely tried to hide the beer behind his back. "I'm, *erm*– I'm just holding them for someone."

"Oh, right." Blake nodded, mildly amused.

"Someone that is eighteen, yeah?"

Daryl nodded.

"Where are you parents?" Blake asked.

Daryl seemed temporarily struck dumb.

"They're on holiday," he said at last. "I've only got a couple of people over. We're not doing anything that bad, promise."

The loud sound of jeering and chatter emanated from inside the house. Blake raised an eyebrow.

"A couple of people, or a couple of football teams?"

Daryl didn't reply. He just stood, looking awkward.

"Look, do me a favour and just turn down the music. I've had a complaint."

"Was it that miserable cow from across the road?" Daryl asked moodily.

"It doesn't matter who it was from," Blake said, though he could hardly disagree with Daryl's sentiments about Imelda. "Just turn it down because if I have to come back here, it'll be with my official head on, and trust me, neither of us want that."

Daryl merely nodded and disappeared sheepishly behind the door.

Blake turned and walked away from the house as the music was drastically lowed in volume. But then, no sooner had his ears registered the silence, another loud blaring noise rang out from across the village. A few moments later, an ambulance came tearing by, its blue lights flashing wildly and siren wailing. It sped round the corner and came to a stop next to the church, which was situated a few yards away from Daryl's house.

Blake frowned and jogged across the road to see what was going on. As he approached the churchyard, he saw the paramedics jumping out of the ambulance, and run into the church. A few moments later, a small throng of distressed people spilled out of the doors.

"What's going on?" Blake asked as he walked towards them.

"Oh, Detective Harte," cried one of the older women, grabbing his arm. "It's Imelda. She's -"

The church door flung open and the two ambulance men bounded out, pulling a stretcher, on top of which was Imelda Atkins, eyes closed and a blanket wrapped around her.

Blake stared in surprise at Imelda's lifeless body as she was hurried towards the ambulance. "What's happened?"

Before anyone could answer, a small, elderly man in cleric's clothing appeared in the church doorway. It was the Reverend Timothy Croydon. Blake, not being a regular visitor in a church had only seen him at the odd village fete that he had frequented, but he had certainly never seen Timothy with such a grave expression on his face.

"Ladies and gentlemen, I know this has all come as a great shock to us all. Perhaps a small prayer from you all tonight would be the correct approach?"

A ripple of murmured agreement passed through the small collective.

Timothy looked sadly down at the ground for a few moments, then spotted Blake. For a moment, he looked like he was unsure as to say anything at all, but then said so quietly that the others couldn't hear, "Detective Harte, isn't it?"

"That's right. Is there anything I can do?"

Timothy hesitated and glanced around. "Not here, would you come inside for a few minutes?"

Blake nodded and passed respectively though the upset congregation to follow Timothy back into the church.

The organ at the other end of the building began to play. The sombre tune, which Blake vaguely recognised from some of the funerals he'd attended over years, reverberated around the church as he wordlessly followed the vicar.

"Just through here," Timothy murmured, leading Blake underneath a set of stone arches, above which were some brilliant pained glass windows depicting a series of saints and angels in blues, reds, and yellows.

Eventually, Blake followed Timothy into the vestry. It was rather cramped with large wooden cupboards around it. Blake could see various coloured robes and cassocks hanging up, and in the far corner was a smaller cupboard that Timothy opened briefly to put away the bible he was carrying. Inside was a silver goblet and a large bottle filled with red liquid, presumably communion wine.

"How can I help?" Blake asked when Timothy again appeared hesitant to say anything.

"Well, I must confess that I don't know exactly that you can," the old vicar said finally. "But, the Lord works in mysterious ways. And when I saw you standing there, I wondered whether I was *supposed* to tell you."

"Tell me what?"

"Imelda. It would appear that she's had a heart attack. They rushed her away fairly quickly, so I pray that she can be revived, but I fear it may be too late."

He paused again, apparently unsure of what he was trying to say.

"Go on?" Blake coaxed.

"Imelda was eighty-one," Timothy continued. "A heart attack is hardly a cause for suspicion or concern at her age, though as far as I was aware, she never had any problems with her heart or blood pressure before."

"Well, heart attacks can be sudden, especially at eighty-one," Blake said, suddenly quite aware that Timothy was of a similar age to Imelda, and not wishing to imply anything morbid.

"Well, quite," Timothy murmured. "But, I'm not

entirely sure she had a heart attack."

Blake frowned. "What do you mean?"

Timothy fiddled with his cassock, looking uncomfortable. "Something very strange is going on inside this church, Detective. I'm sure of it. Imelda's heart seemed to give out when she was in the confessions booth. And in the past few months, that's the third time it's happened." Timothy looked at Blake with the most serious of expressions on his face. "I can't help thinking, Detective, that something altogether more sinister is happening in this church."

CHAPTER
THREE

B lake stared in surprise at the vicar. "Sinister?"

Timothy nodded, apparently regretting his words immediately. "I don't wish to waste any of your time, I know you're a busy man."

"Imelda's in good hands," Blake said. "I'm sure they're doing everything they can to help her."

Timothy shook his head sadly. "I've seen this before, Detective. I am quite certain it's exactly the same thing happening again."

"What do you mean?"

Timothy scratched the back of his head and sighed. "You heard about Nigel Proctor, I suppose?"

Blake had – he was a middle-aged man who had died a few months ago, coincidentally, he realised, of a heart attack.

"Yes. "

"And Mrs Jenkins from Tabernam Road? She died last month."

"Of a heart attack?"

"Quite," Timothy said quietly.

"Well, Nigel Proctor and Mrs Jenkins were both of an age where heart attacks can happen, weren't they?" Blake said, trying to be as tactful as possible. "It does happen."

"But I wonder if you were aware of where they both died?"

Blake thought for a moment. "No, I don't think so."

"It was here. In *this* very church. And not only that, both times it happened, it was in the confessions booth, which is exactly where Imelda was when she keeled over."

Blake stared at the vicar in surprise. "You mean during their confessions?"

"Indeed," Timothy replied seriously. "All three were in the middle of their confessions, and then clutched their chest, came over, quite suddenly very ill, and then collapsed. I recognised it in Imelda so was able to call for an ambulance quite quickly. I fear that even then I was far too late."

Blake stared at the old vicar in bewilderment. "So – just so we're *clear* – you're claiming that Mrs Jenkins, Nigel Proctor, and Imelda Atkins were all sat in the confessions booth of this church, confessed to their sins, and then all immediately had a heart attack?"

"Well, it's not a claim Detective," replied Timothy. "That is exactly what happened."

Blake scratched the back of his head. He wasn't sure if he believed what he was hearing or not. Timothy Croydon wasn't known for bizarre assertions, in fact, the little Blake knew of the man, he had always seemed incredibly on the ball and insightful – skills that no doubt had helped him many times throughout his career in the church. And yet, here he was telling Blake something that made absolutely no sense.

The door to the vestry opened and a man in a long black cassock entered. He smiled inquisitively at Blake as he closed the door behind him.

"Ah, Callum," Timothy said. "This is Detective Sergeant Harte. Detective, this is my grandson and our verger, Callum Dalton."

Blake shook Callum's hand. He had been so distracted from what Timothy had been telling him, he hadn't even noticed that the organ music had stopped.

Callum, who looked to be in his early twenties, with jet-black hair, and a pair of rectangular silver, designer glasses smiled vaguely at Blake, then turned to Timothy. "Everything alright, Granddad?"

Timothy shook his head gravely. "I'm afraid not, Callum. It's happened again."

"Well," Blake put in. "Nothing has really happened –"

"You're kidding." Callum gasped. "Who?"

"Imelda Atkins," Timothy replied, ignoring Blake's attempts to calm the situation. "Same as before. She was giving confession and then seemed to just keel over."

Callum put his hand slowly to his mouth and shook his head in disbelief. "How? I don't know what to say, Granddad, I really don't."

"We've had no word that Imelda has died, Callum," Blake said. "Like I was saying to Timothy, I'm sure she's in the best possible hands."

"Detective," Timothy said, a little sharply. "Over the past four months, three people have sat in that confessions booth and then seemed to just have the life pulled out of them. Imelda was no different. I pray that you're right, and that she manages to make a full recovery, but she acted in exactly the same way as Nigel and Mrs Jenkins. She was in full flow, describing in explicit detail, the way Imelda does, about the things she wished to confess to me, and then the next moment seemed to just collapse. I wish I was mistaken about this, I really do."

"Hey, don't get upset, Granddad," Callum said soothingly, walking towards Timothy and putting his arm around his shoulder. He then looked across at Blake and smiled. "Sorry, but Granddad is right. I can't believe this has happened again. I didn't believe it at first, but there's no other way of saying it. There is definitely something weird going on in this church."

"Detective Harte is the man who was in charge of the case with that young man who got shot in the shed at Halfmile Farm," Timothy said, giving Blake a hopeful look. "I thought if anybody could shine any light on what's going on here, then you could."

Blake held his hands up in surrender. "Okay. Can I take a look at this confessions booth?"

Callum opened the vestry door. "Sure. Come through this way."

Blake turned to follow him out. "Timothy, I promise you, if I find anything remotely suspicious, then I'll make it my top priority to find out what happened."

"Well," Timothy said. "As I say, it does seem quite similar in circumstance to the case you worked on with poor Harrison Baxter." He led Blake, who had ignored the slight feeling of butterflies in his stomach at the mention of Harrison's name, out of the vestry and across the church, Callum leading the way.

"I've been debating coming to see you for a while, but I kept putting it off," the vicar continued. "I do understand what you're saying, I really do. They *could* just have had heart attacks, but every single one of them whilst sat in our confessions booth? You must admit, it does stretch plausibility a little."

Blake had to concede that it did seem bizarre, when it was put to him like that.

The confessions booth was sat against one of the far walls of the church near the font. It was a wooden, rectangular structure with two compartments either side of the entrance door.

Blake opened the door and peered inside. It was dark and gloomy with a metal grill situated between the two compartments and a red velvet curtain draped over the left hand side. "So, how does it work? What happens when someone is giving confession?"

Timothy leant in and pointed to the curtain.

"I, or another priest, sit behind this curtain. The confessor sits in here. Obviously as long as this curtain is drawn, we can't see each other."

Blake looked all around the inside of the priest's side, then went across to the opposite side and sat down, closing the door behind him. "It's not exactly a comforting situation to sit and confess to your deepest and darkest sins, is it?"

Callum leaned in and grinned at Blake through the metal grill. "Well, it certainly seems to work for our parishioners."

Blake glanced at the dashing smile he was being given. Was Callum flirting with him?

"Maybe you should give it a try some time?" Timothy suggested. "We have so many people saying that they feel like a weight has been lifted, whether it's to just get their sins off their chest, or to feel like they've appeased God by confessing."

"I'm atheist," Blake replied apologetically.

He looked around him again, his hands running slowly down the wood around him. There didn't seem to be any kind of openings or ways for anybody else to even get in. The only way it was possible to get to anyone that was sat where Blake was now, was either through opening the door or through the grill.

"I didn't think churches still had these sort of confession booths," Blake replied. "Aren't confessions done more face to face these days?"

"Well, St Abra's has been around for hundreds of years," Timothy said. "The traditional three box set up has always been in place here."

Blake nodded. "Well, I can't find anything out of the ordinary here. And you say they were sat here, talking to you, and then just died?"

"Exactly," Callum replied. "And, not a mark on them. From what Granddad's said, it was as if they just sat there staring, unable to move."

"Almost as if God himself was talking to them,"

Timothy added darkly.

Blake raised a disdainful eyebrow. "Well, whatever has been happening, I think we can be quite sure that it wasn't that."

"And how can you be so sure, Detective?"

Blake climbed out of the confessions box and closed the door behind him and began examining the outer sides. "Because God has a lot of people to keep an eye on, all the Christians, Catholics, and then there's Muslims, Jews, Hindus – doesn't matter if they pay much attention to Him, does it? The whole point is that He is watching over us, am I right?"

"He's got a point, Granddad," Callum replied, grinning again.

"And, out of all those billions of people, I find it hard to believe that He would specifically choose three in Harmschapel to rain His wrath upon. The people in this village have enough difficulty getting their bins collected, I doubt God is that interested. No offence."

The sound of a telephone ringing interrupted Timothy's response. "Excuse me." He glanced irritably at Blake for a moment, then strode towards the vestry.

Callum watched his granddad enter the vestry and close the door sharply behind him. "Don't worry about him. He gets a little sensitive at other people's ideas about God and The Church. For what it's worth, I agree with you." He leant against the door of the confessions booth and looked up at Blake. Despite the long black cassock, Blake couldn't ignore the fact that he was incredibly good looking. He had dark moss green eyes that had a distinct mischievous twinkle about them. "And, don't tell my granddad, but I'm on the same boat as you."

"And which boat would that be?" Blake asked. Half an hour ago, the last place he had expected to find himself was stood in the middle of the village church being flirted with by the verger, but that appeared to be exactly what was happening.

"The atheist boat. I don't believe in any of it. Not really."

Blake was surprised. "Seems a strange career choice for you then. Spending all your time in the church."

Callum shrugged. "The parishioners don't pay any attention to me. I'm just in the background. An extra in the grand scheme of things. It's my granddad they all come to see and listen to – when he's stood at that lectern delivering the word of God, they don't need to know anything about the guy who helps out, holding the crucifix, giving them their bread and wine at communion. They don't need to know that I think it's all a load of crap. I fell on tough times, I lost my last job and things were looking a bit bleak. Granddad helped me out, gave me a position here, and a roof over my head till I find something I'm better suited for. For the time being, this suits me alright. It's all in the performance at the end of the day."

Blake nodded. "And does your granddad know you don't share his views on religion?"

"I think so, but it's sort of an unspoken topic between us," Callum replied. "And while he's saving my bacon like this, I'm happy for it to stay that way."

"So, if you don't buy into the whole word of God thing, then what do *you* think has been going on here?"

Callum shrugged. "I don't know really. I won't lie, it *is* weird. I mean, I hope that it's just a really strange coincidence that two people suffered a fatal heart attack in the way they did. As long as Imelda Atkins doesn't-"

The sound of the vestry door opening and closing cut him off. Timothy walked out, looking pale.

"Are you okay, Granddad?"

"I'm extremely sorry to tell you this, Detective," Timothy said quietly, walking back towards them, his head slightly bowed. "The number has now risen to three. That was John, one of our parishioners on the telephone. Imelda died shortly after they put her in the ambulance. There was nothing they could do for her."

Callum sighed, then looked across at Blake, his eyebrows raised expectantly. "Well, Detective?"

Blake stared at Timothy, his eyes wide. Two people dying in exactly the same way he could accept; three seemed more than suspicious.

"I think it might be time to speak to my boss."

Blake murmured.

CHAPTER
FOUR

W hen Harrison got home, he found carnage awaiting him. His goat, Betty, had been busy while he had been at work. She had managed to get into a drawer containing a lot of papers and documents from when Harrison had sold the farm and moved into the cottage. She had promptly gone about chewing and tearing them up, so that by the time Harrison had arrived home, the whole cottage looked like a blizzard had blown through it, with Betty sat in the middle of it looking extremely pleased with herself.

After a few minutes attempting to salvage some of the documents, Harrison had decided that enough was enough and left her chewing on a bank statement while he walked to The Dog's Tail.

Now, he was sat on his own, nursing a half drunk pint of beer, in some feeble form of celebration for his birthday. He looked around at the small gathering of people in the corner who looked to be having a much better time than he was. It looked like a stag night. The groom to be was downing his fourth pint since Harrison had arrived, cheered on by his friends. He turned away from the noisy group of men and sighed, pushing his pint to the side and resting his head in his hands. This officially was the worst birthday ever.

"You alright, Harrison?"

His thoughts were interrupted by a familiar voice. Mini Patil, one of the officers from the police station was standing behind him, a warm smile on her face.

Harrison sat up straight, attempting to return her friendly expression. "Yeah, I'm alright. Long day. How are you?"

"Oh, I'm alright." Patil said. Harrison glanced at the outfit she was wearing. It was a dark red dress, complete with black tights and matching high heels.

"You look nice," Harrison noted. "Are you going out?"

Patil pulled the bottom of her dress down in a futile attempt to cover her legs

"Oh! Thanks. I wouldn't call it going out, more just..." She hesitated, apparently looking for the right word.

Harrison grinned. "Are you on a date?"

Patil grimaced and then sat down opposite him, leaning in. "Look, I don't know if I'd call it a date. Can you keep a secret?"

Harrison nodded. He liked Patil – she had been just as supportive as Blake during everything that happened at Halfmile Farm, and if he could somehow repay her for her kindness during that difficult time, then he was all too happy to be her confidant.

"You know Matti? Billy Mattison?" Patil said.

"Yeah."

"Well, I'm meeting him here for a drink."

"Are you two an item now, then?"

"No, no, no," Patil said hastily. "I mean, well I think – well, no. I *know* that he probably wants us to be."

"Do you fancy him or not?" Harrison pressed, delighted of the distraction he was now getting from his own problems.

Patil bit her lip and shrugged. "I have absolutely no idea. He's good looking, sweet, funny and we've always got on, but I dunno. I don't know if he's my type, do you know what I mean? I don't want to make some big mistake."

Harrison nodded wistfully. He knew all too well

what it was like to be attracted to the wrong people.

"I mean, you know, don't get me wrong, he's a lovely guy," Patil said, carelessly removing a now dead fly that had landed in Harrison's pint. "But, I don't want to get his hopes up if I don't feel the same way. I mean, he's been like a little brother to me at the station, but outside of work…" She shrugged, sighing. "I just don't know.

"But you think he definitely fancies you?" Harrison asked her.

"Oh, you must be kidding," Patil laughed. "You should have seen him when he asked me for this drink. All nervous and not able to look me in the eye. It was quite adorable really. You on your own tonight?"

Harrison nodded. "Yeah, as per usual."

Patil gave him a sympathetic look. Harrison knew she meant well, but he had had enough sympathy off people in Harmschapel the past few months to last him a lifetime.

"You'll find someone." She smiled. "Good looking lad like you, the men will be fighting to get to you once you put yourself out there."

Harrison gave a nonchalant shrug, then took a sip of his pint.

"And, if all else fails, there's always Sergeant Harte."

Despite trying very hard not to, Harrison swallowed far too much of his drink at the mention of

Blake's name and started coughing.

"You alright?" Patil laughed.

Harrison recovered and wiped his mouth with his sleeve. "Yeah. Just went down the wrong way. What did you say about Bla- erm, Sergeant Harte?"

"Oh, I was only joking. I mean, come on. You and Harte? I know you don't know him that well, but if he's anything like he is at work when he's at home, he's probably got all his CD's filed away alphabetically, and all his underwear ironed and folded in his drawer."

Harrison smiled weakly at her. The thought of anything to do with Blake in underwear made his stomach flip.

"Oh, God," Patil murmured quietly. "He's here."

For a heart stopping moment Harrison thought she meant that Blake had just walked in, but quickly realised by the expression on her face that she meant Mattison. The smell of aftershave had carried all the way to Harrison from the door to the pub before he had even turned round.

"Wow," Harrison said.

Mattison was wearing a dark green shirt that looked like it had been pressed to within an inch of its life. His jeans, similarly, looked absolutely pristine, but Harrison was slightly amused to see that he was wearing completely different shoes. They were the same colour but a closer look betrayed the fact that they had their laces styled in totally opposite ways.

"He's made the effort," Harrison said to Patil, grinning as he watched her bemusement as her eyes travelled down to his odd shoes.

"Hi, Mini," Mattison said nervously as he spotted her. "You look nice."

"Matti," Patil said, tearing her eyes away from his shoes. "So do you. Do you want a drink?"

"No, no. I mean, I *-yeah* I-I do," Mattison stammered. "But, sit down, I'll get them. No worries. What do you want?"

Harrison glanced up at a dark patch that had already started to appear under Mattison's arms. It was almost comforting to witness somebody who was even worse on dates than he was.

"I'll just have a J20, thanks." Patil smiled.

Mattison nodded, obviously trying to work out whether it was alright for him to have alcohol or not. He pulled his wallet out of his pocket and walked to the bar without saying another word.

"Right, I'll leave you to it," Harrison said, pulling his coat on. "Good luck. Bless him, he really wants to make this a good night for you. Let him down gently if you think it's not working."

"I will, don't worry. Have a safe journey home."

Harrison downed the rest of his pint and made his way towards the door of the pub, glancing back at Mattison as he left, who seemed to be receiving some sort of pep talk from Robin, the landlord of the pub. The last thing he saw was Mattison being passed a discreet shot of something as the door closed behind him.

As Harrison made his way home, he thought about what Patil had said to him about getting himself out there to find someone to be with. Living alone for the past few months had felt like some sort of recovery period after the upheaval his life had taken, and he was slowly starting to move on with his life. He wouldn't have the first clue about actually dating anybody though. The idea made him feel almost as anxious as Mattison had looked in the pub. He pulled his phone out of his pocket and loaded up the dating app he had downloaded a few days beforehand. None of the men he saw on there filled him with any particular wanton desire. That was, until, he was suddenly faced with a picture of Blake. He had never seen Blake out of his work clothes before and, though it didn't feel possible, the sight of the man he had thought so much of recently made him feel stronger feelings than ever. These pictures were presumably Blake at his best, and his wavy, mousey coloured hair, his tall physique, and chiselled cheekbones looked better than ever.

He stopped in the street and stared at his phone, which was waiting for him to swipe either left or right on Blake's picture. If Blake *wasn't* interested, then he would surely never find out which way Harrison had swiped. Especially if, as Harrison presumed, Blake had told the app he wasn't interested. After all, it only notified of mutual attraction.

He swiped '*Yes*' on the app, and was disappointed, but not in the slightest bit surprised to see nothing other than the next set of pictures of someone come up. He glanced distastefully for a few moments at the profile picture of '*Teddy Bear*' before closing his app down, thrusting his hands back into his pocket and continuing his journey home.

CHAPTER
FIVE

"Three deaths? In the space of a few months?"

Blake nodded. It was the next morning and he was standing in the doorway of the office of Inspector Royale, his boss at Harmschapel police station, who looked up at him from his desk and scratched his chin, his bushy moustache quivering beneath his nose.

"They all happened in exactly the same way, in the confessions booth of the church. The claim is that all three of them were sat, giving confession, when they seemed to just keel over and die."

"Of heart attacks?" Royale clarified.

"Well, it certainly looks that way, Sir," Blake replied. "I've requested for a post mortem to be performed on Imelda Atkins, but even if it comes back and all seems normal for a woman of her age, I still think it's bloody bizarre."

"Hmm," grunted Royale, clasping his hands together. "Problem is, if forensics don't notice anything suspicious, what do we have to work on? No evidence apart from two clergymen who say that three of their parishioners just died in front of them? It's hardly grounds to warrant opening a murder enquiry, is it?"

"I know," Blake agreed. "And I'd be saying the same if it was just that the three of them had happened to die in the church, I dunno, during a service or something. But Timothy Croydon specifically said that the three of them died while in that confessions booth." Blake looked at his boss seriously. "It just seems like too much of a coincidence. And I don't know about you, Sir, but I've always found that in our line of work, there are very rarely such things as coincidences."

"So, what do you suggest we do then?" said Gardiner, who was sat at his own desk, in the adjourning meeting room, listening to the conversation. "Investigate the church? Follow the nine hundred year old vicar around to make sure he's not working for some sort of gang that targets religious pensioners?"

Blake glared at him. "If you're not going to offer anything helpful, Michael, get on with your work." He turned back to Royale and walked into the office, closing the door behind him. "I don't think I need to tell you this, Sir, but *if* all of these deaths *were* murders, and they were all committed by the same person, that could mean we're looking at a serial killer."

Royale turned slightly pale.

"Trust me," Blake continued. "I hope I'm wrong. I really do. But I think it's something we need to consider. The situation is too suspicious for us not to, at the very least, look in to."

Royale sighed, then nodded. "Alright. I'm trusting you on this one, Blake."

"Thank you, Sir."

"Get as much information as you can find on the three –*victims*-," he hesitated and took a breath. "Then see if there is possibly any connection between them. In the meantime, interview Timothy Croydon and any other witnesses to any of the deaths."

Blake didn't really need to be told any of that, but he politely nodded. "Yes, Sir."

"Carry on," Royale said.

Blake walked out of the office and towards

Gardiner's desk. "Right, Michael. Come with me."

Gardiner glanced up at Blake disdainfully. "Why?"

Blake was in no mood for his bolshie attitude. "Because I've asked you to. That should be all you need to hear. If you've got any problems with that, Inspector Royale's office is just there. If not, can you get the keys to one of the cars and meet me outside? Thank you."

He didn't wait for a response, instead picking up his jacket from his own desk and striding outside.

Blake and Gardiner had had a somewhat strained working relationship ever since Blake had arrived in Harmschapel. It had become clear to Blake very quickly that Gardiner had been hoping to be promoted to the position that Blake now held, and as a result, Gardiner was often nothing short of awkward and antagonistic to work with. While they had once had a brief moment of reconciliation, where Gardiner had confessed to Blake that he was going through a messy divorce on account of his wife having an affair with his brother, he still seemed to be just a naturally prickly person. More recently, Blake had heard on the grapevine that Gardiner's wife was trying to get as much money out of the divorce as possible, leading to Gardiner becoming more hostile to all around him than ever.

Blake was a firm believer that once any officer crossed the threshold to the station that their personal problems were left at the door. Gardiner didn't seem to agree, and he would be damned before he would let a much younger officer, his superior or not, tell him otherwise.

By the time Gardiner had stormed outside with the keys to one of the cars, Blake had had a few sucks on his ecig, which he had fortunately remembered to charge before work that morning, and was in a more reasonable frame of mind.

"So, where are we going?" Gardiner asked him as they climbed into the car.

"To the church," Blake replied. "We're going to talk to anybody who works there and see if they can shed any light on what's been happening."

Gardiner pulled the car out of the station car park and said, "I'm sorry but I really don't see how three elderly people dying from a heart attack warrants any form of police investigation. So their tickers gave out when they were getting themselves worked up about any sins they think they committed – why does that need us to get involved?"

"Well, we'll soon find out, won't we?" Blake replied bluntly.

They travelled in silence for a few more minutes, with the only sound in the car coming from the radio, which was in the middle of a weather report, warning of thunder and lightning coming from the south. Blake switched it off and crossed his arms.

"Any chance of me getting any co-operation from you with this?"

"I'm allowed an opinion, aren't I?" Gardiner grunted in reply

"Yes, but you're my sergeant. Second in command. That's what I need, not somebody acting like a hormonal teenager."

"I'm not acting like-"

"Well, yes actually you are," interrupted Blake. "I don't expect every single instruction I give you to be greeted with arguments and sulking. Come on, Michael – you're a *grown man*. You know what's expected of you."

"Really making your mark at this station, aren't you?" snapped Gardiner, slamming the indicator down to turn left.

"Hardly. I think it's more that things are still difficult at home, aren't they?"

"I don't want to talk about it."

"Fine. Then in that case, brighten up."

Gardiner didn't reply.

When they arrived at the church, the sun had disappeared behind a huge gathering of clouds, and as a result, despite it being morning, the churchyard looked gloomy and unwelcoming. The black metal gate squeaked loudly as Blake opened it, shattering the otherwise eerie silence.

As they walked towards the front entrance, the door was opened from within, and a woman stepped out, who smiling happily when she noticed Blake.

"Oh, hello, darling!"

"Evening, Jacqueline," Blake said with a smile. "Didn't expect to see you here."

The landlady to his house shrugged modestly. "I'm actually Catholic. It's been a while since I've been to church though." She then spotted Gardiner, who was staring at her fiercely hair sprayed beehive with a raised eyebrow. Jacqueline straightened up and stuck her chest out slightly with what she clearly believed to be with some degree of subtlety. "I've been sinning. Regularly."

Blake cleared his throat. "I don't think you've met Sergeant Gardiner, have you Jacqueline? Michael, this is my landlady."

Gardiner nodded curtly as Jacqueline held her hand out. "Delighted to meet you, Sergeant."

Gardiner glanced at her hand and clasped it briefly.

"Well," Blake said, in an attempt to break the uncomfortable moment. "Things to do Jacqueline. I'll see you around?"

"Yes, of course, darling," Jacqueline said. "Nice to meet you, Sergeant." And with a flirtatious look up and down of Gardiner, she walked away, the scent of her perfume hanging in the air.

"I wouldn't worry about it." Grinned Blake. "She flirted with me incessantly before she found out I was gay. She's harmless."

Gardiner grunted and straightened his jacket. "Well, she's not keeled over from committing sins has she?"

"It would take more than a vengeful and angry God to finish off Jacqueline." Blake chuckled. "Come on."

Inside the church, the light was far dimmer than it had appeared outside. Candles were placed around the building in various stages of their lifespan, and the place seemed to be fairly empty, until Blake spotted somebody kneeling at the altar beneath the statues and crucifix displayed over the front of the church.

He slowly walked towards the figure, who had their head bowed and seemed to be in deep prayer. After a minute or so, Blake cleared his throat, quietly but loud enough for the figure to hear. Their head snapped up and turned to stare at the new arrivals.

It was a woman in her late fifties. She had frizzy grey hair, and a white dog collar placed in the centre of her neck through her black shirt. Her cold blue eyes narrowed.

"Can I help you?" she asked sharply.

"Ah, I'm sorry," Blake said, pulling his ID from his pocket. "I didn't mean to startle you."

"You didn't."

"D.S Blake Harte, this is Sergeant Michael Gardiner. We were hoping to speak to the reverend Timothy Croydon?"

The woman stood up and walked towards him. "Father Croydon's not here at the moment. He went into town earlier this morning. I presume, that this is to do with the deaths of three of our parishioners?"

"Yes, that's right," Blake said. "What did you say your name was?"

"I didn't."

There was a brief pause. Once Blake gathered that she wasn't planning on filling it with a more helpful response to his question, he asked, "Well, could you?"

"Jennifer Greene. I'm one of the reverends here."

"Miss Greene recently became ordained," Gardiner said from behind Blake. "I think it was you that was in the paper some weeks ago."

"Oh?" Blake asked. "What was that about?"

"I wrote a column," replied Jennifer. "About the backlash I'd faced in the Catholic community about becoming a priest."

"Oh, I see," Blake said gravely. "I take it it's still a struggle for women to become priests in the Catholic Church?"

"It is. The stigma attached is still very much a real thing. And it's not helped by some of the woman within the community, either. Though you're not here to ask about my views on that, are you?"

"Were you a witness to any of the incidents that took place here over the past few months?" Blake asked her.

"I called the ambulance for the first one, Nigel Proctor."

"And that was about, what, six months ago now?"

Jennifer nodded. "I saw him go into the confessions booth. Father Croydon was inside waiting for him. About five minutes or so passed. I was at the lectern, selecting a bible reading for the next service that evening. I looked up as the Father suddenly rushed out. He shouted for me to call for help."

"Which you did straight away?" Blake clarified.

"Obviously. But, of course, by the time the ambulance had arrived, he was already dead."

Blake chose to ignore the defensive way she was answering his questions and pressed on. "Is there anything you can tell us about Nigel?"

"Such as?"

"Do you know whether he had any previous heart problems or any general health concerns that may have led him to have a heart attack?"

"Why would I know that?" Jennifer sniffed. "I'm a priest, not a doctor. All I know is that he was a man in his late sixties who *could* have had a heart attack. I knew him enough to nod at in the street, pass the time of day, but other than that, not a great deal."

"Do you know what he did for a living?" Blake

asked.

"I think he was a caretaker at the college. I know he worked there anyway and I believe it was in some form of janitor position."

"What about Mrs Jenkins? Do you know what her first name was?"

"Patricia. Or Pat to her friends. Not that she had many. She preferred to be called Mrs Jenkins by everyone as a rule. She was quite close to Imelda Atkins though. The pair of them had been coming to this church for years and they always sat together. I wasn't very keen on either of them, I'm afraid."

"And why was that?"

"They were quite vocal about my becoming a priest here." Jennifer replied sharply. "Imelda in particular had absolutely no problem in saying how she felt about a lot of things and that was no exception."

"Yes, we're quite familiar with Imelda's complaining," Blake said, glancing at Gardiner who merely rolled his eyes.

"I'm sure. My column in the paper was in response to their complaints actually," Jennifer said proudly. "They had made a big song and dance about it, once they'd got wind of my inauguration, to the point where they had composed a letter, signed by as many people around the village as they could muster, and sent it to the bishop. Fortunately, it was all to no avail. But any service I was ever giving, you could be certain that neither of them would be attending. Imelda missed a funeral of someone she'd known for years because I was the vicar for it. Nasty spirited woman. Can't say I'll miss her or Patricia Jenkins I'm afraid."

Gardiner cleared his throat and folded his arms. "So, if someone wants to confess their sins to someone-"

"That someone being God," corrected Jennifer briskly.

"What happens?" Gardiner asked, ignoring her. "I mean, what's the procedure?"

Blake was glad that he had decided to get involved at last.

"You make an appointment, and arrange a time. A confession can take a couple of minutes or go over ten."

"So," Blake said. "In all three cases, they went into that booth and within ten minutes had all died. Is that what you're saying?"

Jennifer gave a humourless chuckle, indicating to the stained glass window above the large golden crucifix. "Do you know what I was doing when you interrupted me?"

"I assumed you were praying."

"Exactly. There is a reason I have fought so hard to become a priest. It's not just about the principle of fighting off discrimination about women holding my position in the church. It's because I know that my role in life is to serve God, and to pass His word on to those that believe. I hope that leads me to living a long and happy life because I do what I was put on this earth to do. I follow the rules. Some people clearly don't. And as you can see, I'm still here."

"You mean you think that those people died because God decided it?" Blake asked, glancing at Gardiner, who was staring at Jennifer with a look of bewilderment.

Jennifer held her hands out and shrugged as if to imply that her point was obvious. "Now, was there anything else? I have work to do today."

Blake considered for a moment, but decided that he was unlikely to get anything remotely helpful out of her at this stage. "If you could just tell Timothy that we wanted to speak to him."

"Certainly."

Blake turned and walked away from the altar with Gardiner closely behind. "But, I think it's quite likely we're going to need to see you again, Jennifer. We'll be in touch."

Jennifer nodded curtly, then turned and walked away to the back of the church.

When she had gone, Blake turned to Gardiner. "Well?"

"Well," Gardiner replied flatly. "I think the only suspects you have so far are high cholesterol and God."

"So, you think this is all still some strange coincidence?"

"Oh come on," said Gardiner. "Look at that confessions booth." He pointed to the structure on the other side of the building, which looked cold and murky in the shadows. "You can't seriously expect me to believe that three people were somehow murdered in there. Look at it."

"Go on then, take a look!" Blake told him.

Gardiner sighed and strode over to the booth, with Blake closely behind him. "What you're saying is ridiculous. One box for the vicar, another for the confessor. There's a single grill between them." He gave Blake a look of derision and grasped the handle to the side where the confessor would sit. "What do you expect to find in here?"

He pulled the door open but before he could look inside, he stumbled backwards as someone fell out of it. Blake stared as the body landed on the ground and stared back up at him, lifeless.

"Oh my God," Blake murmured.

Lying on the ground was a young man. He couldn't have been any older than eighteen. Blake raised his hand to his mouth as he realised who it was. He had only seen him the night before, clutching a beer can and looking so full of life.

It was Daryl Stuarts.

CHAPTER
SIX

H arrison's nose itched as he wiped the dusty top shelf with a damp cloth. He threw the cloth down to the ground, and sneezed loudly, groaning as he did so. Jai Sinnah, the owner of the shop where Harrison had worked for the past few months was on holiday, and had left Harrison a list of jobs that he had insisted wouldn't take him long to complete. By the time Harrison had gotten to job twenty-two, he had come to the conclusion that Jai was a liar, and judging by the amount of jobs he had started that didn't even need particularly doing, a fussy one at that.

Once he had finished wiping the shelf clean, he began putting the biscuits back haphazardly on the shelf, deciding he would tidy them up before he left that evening. His mind wandered to the stag night he had seen the night before. He wondered if the groom to be, even if he was hung-over, was having a better time than he was at that moment. As he placed the last biscuit packet on the shelf, it unbalanced the rough pile he had made from the bottom, sending them all cascading to the floor again.

Harrison swore loudly, not noticing somebody appearing behind him.

"Well, I quite like broken biscuits anyway."

He looked up to see a good looking man with jet-black hair and dark green eyes smiling back at him.

Harrison had been so distracted, he hadn't even heard him come in. "Sorry, I was miles away. Can I help you?"

"I just wanted to get this," replied the man, holding up a bottle of water. "Harrison, isn't it?"

"Yeah, that's right." After everything that had happened, Harrison had grown more than used to people he didn't recognise knowing who he was, even excusing for a village the size of Harmschapel. He stood up and quickly hurried behind the till, wiping the dust off from his uniform as he did so. "That's eighty pence please."

The man handed over a pound coin. "I'm Callum. I work at the church."

"Oh, are you Timothy Croydon's grandson?" Harrison asked, tapping the till and passing Callum his change.

"Yeah, that's right. Granddad said that he had spoken to you the other week. I know it's none of my business, sorry. But is it true? What everyone's saying? You know what gossip around this village can be like. I didn't know whether it had all been blown out of proportion."

"Whatever you've heard about me is probably true." Harrison sighed.

Callum's mouth fell open. "You mean you *do* turn into a werewolf at the full moon? Wow."

Harrison stared at him in confusion for a moment until he realised Callum was joking and laughing. "Yeah. I try to eat at least one gossiping Harmschapel resident every time."

Callum grinned. "It's good that you can laugh about it at least though, seriously. If it all *is* true, then it sounds really awful. I'm sorry."

Harrison shrugged awkwardly. "Not a lot I can do about it now. New start for me, I guess."

Callum took a sip of his water, then scratched the back of his head. "Look, this is going to sound weird, I know. But my parents aren't around either. My dad died when I was three and my mum just up and went after that, leaving me with just my granddad. I know it's not the same thing at all, but I know what it's like to practically be an orphan. If you ever want to talk, let stuff off your chest, I've been told I'm a good listener."

"You sound just like your granddad," Harrison said lightly. A few weeks ago, Timothy had stopped Harrison in the street, assuring him that if he ever wanted to tell him and God all about his problems, then both of them would be only too happy to listen. Harrison had politely declined.

"Yeah, but I don't mean with God listening in. That's just my job. I mean, you know. Human to human. Or human to werewolf. I promise I won't try and convert you."

Harrison's first thought was to say the same thing to Callum as he had to his Granddad and as he had to so many other apparently well-meaning people over the past few months. But when he thought about it, Callum actually sounded like he would be able to offer some genuine and heartfelt advice. The truth was that Harrison hadn't really had anybody to talk to for a couple of months, and he now had the opportunity to, at the very least, socialise with somebody who didn't seem to just want to get a good story to gossip about with their friends.

"Are you free anytime soon?" He found himself saying.

Callum smiled and nodded. "I'm not doing anything tonight. How about The Dog's Tail at seven?"

"Sounds good to me."

"Great. I'll see you there." Callum gave Harrison one last dashing grin and walked out of the shop clutching his bottle of water.

Harrison watched him leave, realising he was smiling; A genuine, nervous, but happy smile. He wasn't quite sure whether he had just organised a date or just a meeting with a potential new friend but either way, one thing he did know was that he was really looking forward to it.

The door to the shop opened again, and a much less attractive sight walked in. Mattison looked awful. His hair was messy, his uniform was creased and unkempt, and he had bags underneath his exhausted eyes.

"Matti?"

Mattison glanced up at Harrison and shook his head. "I need something for my head please, Harrison. And also a new identity if you sell them."

"Top shelf by the bathroom stuff. Are you alright?"

Mattison slouched to the back of the shop, pulling an energy drink out of the chiller on his way past. He stared vaguely at the medication shelf before finally selecting a packet of extra strength aspirin. "I'm too hung-over to talk about it. It was you in The Dog's Tail last night wasn't it?" He chucked the aspirin on the counter and exhaled, possibly to try and stop himself from vomiting.

"Yeah, for a bit. Did you have a good time? How did your night with Mini go?"

"How much are they?" Mattison asked, ignoring his question. "I just want to pretend last night never happened."

"Two quid altogether."

Mattison pulled out a five-pound note from his wallet and passed it to Harrison.

"Dare I ask?" Harrison grinned, putting the transaction through the till and passing Mattison his change.

Mattison groaned loudly before roughly pulling the aspirin packet open, quickly swallowing two of the small white tablets with the help of the energy drink.

"I got drunk. Drunker than I should have done. It was Robin's fault. I was really nervous and he kept giving me these shots to calm my nerves. I'm pretty sure that it was Sambuca. After about my fifth, it's all a bit of a blur. All I know is that I made an absolute idiot out of myself." He took another swig of his energy drink, stopping when he heard his phone ringing in his pocket.

"Oh God," he muttered as he looked at the screen. He swiped his thumb on the screen and put it tentatively to his ear. "Hello, Sir. I'm nearly at the station now, I just –"

He stopped, listening intently and glanced at Harrison, before nodding at him in thanks and hurrying out of the shop. Harrison watched him leave and felt a wave of sympathy. If Mattison had felt the same way about Patil as Harrison did about Blake he couldn't imagine how awful Mattison must be feeling if he had ruined the date, purely by getting drunk.

Still, Harrison told himself, he needed to stop thinking so much about Blake. It was never going to happen, although it had certainly been a long time since he had received any sort of attention like that, he did get the feeling that Callum wanted to meet him with more than just a friendly chat in mind. It could be the perfect distraction from Blake and right now, Harrison couldn't think of anything he needed more than a good distraction.

CHAPTER
SEVEN

T hroughout his career, Blake had seen quite the number of dead bodies, but there was something undeniably unnerving about watching the forensics team examine a body in a dimly lit church. He glanced down at Daryl's body from where he was sat, unable to comprehend how this had happened to somebody so young. He was seventeen, a college student with his whole life in front of him. His parents were out of the country, completely unaware that they didn't have a son anymore. Whoever had done this had taken away somebody's child. There was no doubt in Blake's mind that this was murder.

Sharon Donahue, the forensic pathologist whom he had gotten to know since he had arrived in Harmschapel, walked over to him and pulled her facemask down.

"I've got to be honest Blake. I'll be buggered if I know what's happened to him. Obviously we'll have to get him back and take a closer look, but from what we can see there's not a mark on him. Judging by the level of rigor, I'd say he's been dead no longer than about ten hours. Other than that…" She shook her head and sat down beside him. She looked over at him, and gave him a sympathetic look. "I know. Me too. He's too young."

Blake didn't say anything. He just exhaled in an attempt to pull himself together, and pulled his ecig out of his pocket.

"I don't think you're allowed to smoke that in here, Blake," Sharon said gently.

"Yeah, well you're not supposed to murder anybody either," Blake replied curtly, giving the ecig just the one suck before putting it back in his pocket. "How long before I can get a report on what's happened to him?"

"I'll try and get him done as quickly as I can," Sharon said. "You know it takes as long as it takes if I don't know what killed him."

Blake nodded. "Have you finished with Imelda Atkins?"

"Funnily enough," Sharon said. "I sent the report to you first thing this morning. Didn't realise I'd be seeing you though obviously. Nothing out of the ordinary for a woman in her eighties. From what we found, nothing would argue against some form of cardiac arrest."

"So, a heart attack?" Blake murmured. "But he's a seventeen year old boy. From what I know about him, he plays football, rugby. He shouldn't have had any issues with his heart."

"I'll get him looked at as soon as I can," Sharon said. "That confessions booth is all yours now, we're done. We couldn't find anything wrong with it. It's absolutely covered in about a hundred or so different sets of fingerprints, but what else would you expect?"

The church door opened behind them and Mattison walked in.

"Sorry I'm late, Sir," he said sheepishly as he approached.

Blake glanced up at him. "No offence, Matti, but you look god awful. Are you hung-over?"

Mattison shook his head quickly. "I just didn't get very much sleep last night, Sir."

Blake didn't believe him, but now was hardly the time to interrogate him any further. "I'm guessing you didn't have time to iron that uniform this morning?

Do me a favour and keep your coat on, then get outside and make sure than nobody unauthorised comes in."

Mattison nodded and looked across at Daryl's body, his mouth falling open. "Oh my God, is that Daryl Stuarts?"

"How do you know him?"

"He was a few years below me at school. I think I left just as he was starting," replied Mattison, looking even paler than he had than when he had first walked in.

"His parents will need informing." Blake sighed. "Mini, can you get onto that please?"

Patil wandered over from where she had be talking to one of the forensics team. She gave Mattison a peculiar look that Blake hadn't seen between them before, then walked out of the door, clutching her mobile without another word.

Blake frowned as she left. "What's wrong with her?"

Mattison gave an unconvincing shrug. "I'm not sure. I'll just go and sort outside out."

He shuffled uncomfortably away. Blake watched him leave then turned to Gardiner.

"Where is she?"

"She's in the vestry," said Gardiner.

"Right."

He strode across the church to the vestry door

and flung it open. Out of anybody he had spoken to so far regarding the strange events at St Abra's church, Jennifer Greene had appeared the most callous and cold about what had happened and Blake wasn't about to let it continue.

"Right, Jennifer," he said, barging in. Jennifer jumped from behind the desk on the other side of the vestry. "I think it's fair to say there is absolutely no doubt that we are in the middle of a murder enquiry. I'm going to ask you what you know about anything that's been going on here, and please don't think for a second that I'm going to take '*God did it*' as a suitable answer."

Jennifer didn't respond.

"Let's start with Daryl Stuarts. Do you know him?"

Jennifer shook her head. "He isn't, well, wasn't a regular parishioner, if that's what you mean."

"So, he wasn't religious?"

"Well, I don't know whether he was or not," Jennifer replied. "But if he was he didn't practice here. I don't know his family, I wouldn't know him to nod to on the street, never mind have a full conversation about where he stood on matters of the church."

"Where were you last night?" Blake asked her, crossing his arms and leaning against one of the cabinets.

"I was at home mostly. I live alone before you ask,

so no, there's nobody to verify what I'm saying."

"At home '*mostly*'?" Blake repeated. "Where else were you, say – about ten, eleven PM?"

"I visited one of my parishioners."

"That late?"

"It's not just the elderly who come to church, Detective," Jennifer said curtly.

"Who was it you went to see?"

"Why do you need to know that?"

"Because they may be the only person who can confirm your whereabouts when Daryl Stuarts was killed," Blake said, his tone serious.

"I very much doubt that who I visited last night will be able to tell you anything remotely useful whatsoever."

"Why not?"

"Because I visited them in hospital. She's not very well at all. The drugs they have her on don't exactly make her the most lucid of people."

Blake nodded. "I'm sorry to hear that. Which hospital was this?"

"St Anne's Royal. It's about a thirty minute or so drive away," Jennifer replied quietly.

Blake paused for a moment then continued.

"What time did you get home?"

"About a quarter to eleven," she said. "I knew I had an early start this morning so I went straight to bed when I got in. I didn't leave my house again till around eight this morning."

"Let's talk some more about Imelda Atkins and Patricia Jenkins," Blake continued, pulling a stool towards him to sit opposite her. "You said they gave you a hard time about becoming a priest here?"

"They did," Jennifer mumbled, frowning. "But I hope you're not suggesting that I killed them for it."

"I'm merely trying to gather the facts," Blake said steadily. "If everybody who died in that confessions booth was murdered, then it stands to reason that they were killed by somebody who thinks that they deserved to die. Doesn't it?"

Jennifer, with some apparent reluctance, nodded.

"So," Blake continued. "You said that Imelda and Patricia were boycotting your services?"

"Yes. And they managed to get quite a few others to do the same. It was vicious talk mostly. Going around saying how I wasn't fit to be ordained, trying to find out as much as they could about my past to prove their point. I imagine it's how politicians feel when their opponents dig up sordid secrets from their pasts. They made sure the rest of the village knew about any skeletons they found.

"And what skeletons did they find?"

"Nothing relevant to your investigation, I assure you."

"Sorry, Jennifer, but that's up to me to decide."

Jennifer stood up and opened one of the cabinets

behind Blake, busying herself by tidying up some of the communion goblets. "Well, if you must know they came across an ex of mine. We parted ways just before I was ordained."

"What's wrong with that?"

"My ex-partner was standing on my doorstep dropping off some of my things that I had left at her house."

"*Her* house? I see," Blake said gently. "And they put two and two together?"

"We ended things amicably enough," Jennifer said, repositioning the same goblet for the second time, appearing to want to avoid Blake's gaze. "Some relationships just don't work out. Nina is atheist. The struggles I had becoming ordained were putting a strain on our relationship, and quite frankly, my work was more important. There's still love between us. She kissed me goodbye when she dropped my things off, and unfortunately Imelda chose that moment to come round the corner."

"I'm sorry, but I have to ask this," Blake said, scratching the back of his head. "With all this against you, why would you want to work in an establishment that not only doesn't accept your sexuality, but also your gender?"

Jennifer closed the cabinet sharply and turned to look at Blake, a serious expression on her face. "One day, the Catholic church will progress to the point where that isn't important. Maybe that day isn't today. I am, after all, only one person. But I believe the word of God just as much as anybody else in my position. I doubt I'll ever marry, I don't think I'm in a position where I can, or should. But, it all has to start somewhere. Catholic teachings have progressed as far as my sexuality is concerned. It's still seen as immoral, but at the same time, the thinking now is that we must be treated with respect, compassion, and sensitivity." She sat down again and sighed deeply. "There's a long way to go. A *very* long way. There are many that believe that homosexuality is a trial that we somehow need to fight through. But the tide is turning."

Blake had to admit that he found what she was saying quite inspiring. He remembered when he had first joined the police force, and had been worried about his own sexuality. When he eventually came out to his colleagues, he had experienced some bigotry and discrimination. The majority of it had just been banter that he quickly learnt to laugh at. He couldn't imagine a life where he wasn't a police officer – so why, he thought, should Jennifer's life be any different?

"Okay, Jennifer. I think we'll leave it there. I'll be wanting to speak to you again though."

"I see."

Blake stood up and went to walk out of the vestry.

"Detective?"

Blake stopped at the door. Jennifer stood up and

picked up a bible that was on the desk. "I'd suggest to you that you opened your mind a bit. There's absolutely no guarantee that you'll find whoever is doing this. Maybe then, you'll start to appreciate that there might just be other forces at work. Not everything can be worked out by a cold and cynical mind."

Blake narrowed his eyes but didn't say anything. He merely nodded a goodbye to her and walked out of the church.

CHAPTER
EIGHT

Harrison sipped the last of his pint and put it down on the table, a little harder he had intended. "So, I sold the farm. My Dad said that I could keep the money from it after everything that had happened-"

"Which it sounds like you deserved. It was the least he could do," Callum said, nodding in agreement.

"Well." Harrison shrugged. "Either way, I bought the cottage, and now it's just me and Betty."

Callum raised an eyebrow, grinning. "Betty?"

"Oh," Harrison said sheepishly. "Betty's my goat."

"Betty?" Callum repeated, chuckling.

Harrison started laughing. He wasn't sure if it was that funny or whether his third pint had started to go to his head. "Yeah, Betty. I was a fan of Betty Boop as a kid, I don't know why."

"Betty the goat." Callum grinned. "That's the best thing I've ever heard."

Harrison laughed again, enjoying a euphoric sensation he hadn't felt in such a long time.

They had been at the pub for about an hour now and since they'd sat down, Harrison had found himself deep in conversation with a man he had met only a few hours ago. Something about Callum was open, understanding, and incredibly easy to talk to. He had even bought Harrison all three of the pints he had drunk, and as a result, any anxiety had been quickly dissolved.

"So, go on," Harrison said, leaning on the table with his arms crossed. "You've listened to my ridiculous life for long enough." They looked at each other and laughed. "Tell me about you. It sounds like you've had a pretty rough time of it."

Callum nodded. "Yeah. You could say that."

"You said your dad died when you were three?"

Again, Callum nodded. "And then, Mum just up and left. Granddad didn't tell me the full story till I was eighteen. Mum and me had been staying round his house for Christmas. I was put to bed, all excited 'cause Santa was coming. Apparently Granddad woke up to a note saying how it was all too much, how she could never give me what I needed in life, and that she was sorry. I've not heard from her since. I don't remember any of it, obviously being three, but Granddad says I just spent the whole of that Christmas day in floods of tears, and I didn't stop crying till Boxing Day."

"That's so sad," Harrison said, genuinely stunned. "And you've got absolutely no idea where she is?"

"Nope. Granddad thinks she probably disappeared to London somewhere – apparently there was a guy who lived there that she was seeing on and off. Other than that, not a clue."

"Do you ever think of going to look for her?"

"Yeah." Callum smiled. "Some nights I just lie there thinking of all the different scenarios of me just turning up on her doorstep. I play them out in my head in explicit detail, right down to what she's wearing, and what her front door looks like. She either welcomes me back with open arms, or tells me to get lost because she walked out for a reason." Callum's eye line drifted off, as if he was picturing himself being reunited with his mother. "The only thing that stops me from actually trying to find her is if it's the scenario where she isn't interested. I'm not sure I could handle it."

There was a brief pause as he pulled himself out of

his daydream and back to the real world.

"Anyway," he continued. "A couple of years ago, I managed to get a job working at the college in Clackton as a lab technician. I've always been interested in science, and that sort of thing. Then, a few months back, they let me go. Apparently they *'didn't have the money in the department to make the position financially viable anymore.'* That sucked." He took a sip from his drink and swallowed, his expression turning momentarily bitter. "But then, Granddad got me the job working at the church, and I've been there ever since. Feel like I'm kind of treading water at the moment, but at least I've got money and a roof over my head."

"I guess in a weird way I'm quite lucky," Harrison said. "My dad let me keep the money from selling the farm. I don't need that much. Just to keep me and Betty fed."

Callum chuckled again. "Betty."

"What's wrong with Betty?" Harrison grinned.

"Don't worry about it." Callum said, downing the rest of his drink. "If I'd been you, then I'd be the proud owner of a goat called Thomas the Tank Engine. Doesn't have quite the same ring to it."

Harrison laughed, probably a lot harder than was needed, but he didn't care. He was having more fun.

"Thanks for tonight," he said. "I've really enjoyed it. Makes up for my crappy birthday yesterday."

Callum's eyes widened. "It was your birthday? You're kidding. What did you do?"

"Nothing."

"Nothing at all?"

Harrison shook his head.

"Right then," Callum said firmly, standing up and pulling his jacket on. "Get your coat on. You're coming with me."

"Why? Where are we going?"

"Never mind the questions." Callum grinned, picking up the two empty glasses. "Just do as you're told. As of right now, it's your birthday again."

He placed the empty glasses on the bar, stood up and pulled his coat on. Whatever Callum had planned, Harrison decided he owed it to himself to see where the night took him. Callum thanked Robin and then led Harrison out of the pub.

"Right," Callum said, checking his phone. "We've got about ten minutes till the last bus."

"The bus?"

Callum turned to him and flashed a grin that was impossible to argue with. "When was the last time you let you let your hair down and enjoyed yourself?"

"Erm…" Harrison paused, not because he was trying to remember when, more that he was attempting to come up with a convincing enough lie that would make him sound like he had more of social life than he did.

"It doesn't matter," Callum interrupted. "We're doing it tonight. From this point onwards, when anybody asks you what you did for your twenty-third birthday, you went out and you got ridiculously drunk, and had the time of your life. Clear?"

Harrison was too stunned to say anything so he merely nodded.

"Good. Come on then."

And without another word, Callum grabbed Harrison's wrist and they ran as fast as they could to the bus stop on the other side of the village.

CHAPTER
NINE

"Thank you for coming this evening everybody," Blake said, as he finished wiping the whiteboard in the meeting room clean and turned to his audience.

He glanced up at the clock on the wall. It was a large digital one that Mandy Darnwood had won at the bingo, and had had no place for in her own home. It was just after ten. It was going to be a long evening.

Mattison kicked open the door, carrying a large tray of steaming mugs. Blake had requested the second they got back to the station that everybody had a caffeinated drink near them. As the newest and youngest officer, it had fallen to Mattison to prepare them. Blake remembered a time, one that felt like a hundred and twenty years ago, when he had been the one on drink duty.

"Okay," Blake began. "In the past six months, St Abra's church appears to have been the location of three unexplained deaths. Tonight, that number became four." He picked up a series of photographs, and stuck them up on the whiteboard. "We have Nigel Proctor, Patricia Jenkins, Imelda Atkins, and as of this morning, more than likely last night, Daryl Stuarts." He paused as he wrote each of the victim's names underneath their pictures. Daryl's graphic photograph gave him a twinge of sadness. It was the only one that had been taken by forensics. All the others were pictures that had been provided by the families or friends and showed their occupants smiling happily, or in Imelda's case just contentedly staring at the camera.

"Let's establish a few facts before we start theorising anything. Do we have precise ages for the first three?"

"Yes, Sir," Patil said, promptly producing her notebook. "Nigel Proctor, sixty-nine, Patricia Jenkins, seventy-five, and Imelda Atkins was eighty-one."

Blake scribbled the three ages next to their names. "And as we know, Daryl Stuarts was only seventeen."

He wrote Daryl's age, then tapped the board with the end of his pen. "So, why am I asking about their ages?"

"They all appear to have died from some form of heart attack," Mattison said. "The first three are all at an age where that's more likely, but Daryl was seventeen and so-"

"So he shouldn't be dropping dead from a cardiac arrest, exactly," finished Blake. "Now, obviously until we get Daryl's post-mortem results back, we won't know if he's died the same way as all the others, but given that he was found in exactly the same way as the other three, in that confessions booth, without a scratch on him, it's not exactly a leap to the conclusion that he is in some way, connected. Everyone with me so far?"

There was a general murmur of assertion from around the room. Gardiner, who was sat at his desk at the back of the room with his arms crossed, cleared his throat.

"Yes, Michael?"

"We don't know that every single one of those people have been murdered, do we?"

"Oh, come on," Mattison piped up. "How can they not have been?"

"No, Matti – he's actually right," Blake said, sighing heavily, holding up the report that Sharon had sent him. "Because, with two of them already in the ground with no questions asked, and one post-mortem report telling me that a woman in her eighties died from a heart attack, we do not actually have any remotely concrete forensic evidence to tell us that any of these three died from anything other than natural causes." He threw the report back down on the desk and turned back to the board. "But, what we do have is four deaths that are connected alone by that confessions booth. Witness statements?"

Mattison put his coffee down that he had been in the middle of sipping, and picked up a report in front of him. "So, according to Jennifer Greene, Nigel Proctor went into the confessions booth at approximately ten forty-five on the morning of Sunday, eighth of April this year. He appeared fine when he went in, but around ten minutes later she was told to call an ambulance because he was '*clutching his chest and crying out in pain.*'"

"Twenty minutes later, the ambulance arrives, but he's sadly no longer with us," Blake added. "I spoke to Timothy Croydon and asked him about Imelda and Patricia. Both exactly the same story."

Mattison continued, "According to the vicar, they were both sat in that confessions booth, in the middle of a sentence before very quickly coming over extremely ill. Then, just like Nigel Proctor, they became unresponsive, and a few minutes later had died."

"Okay, so my thought is that we leave Daryl

Stuarts out of the picture for a minute," Blake said, removing Daryl's photograph from the board, placing it on the desk in front of him. "Let's concentrate on the first three deaths. Because if we *are* going with the idea that all three of these people were murdered, then it puts Daryl in a completely different ball park, doesn't it?"

"Why?" Gardiner asked dryly.

"Well, isn't it obvious?" Patil exclaimed, turning round to look at Gardiner.

Gardiner glared at her. "Not to me."

"Oh come on, Sarge, the first three, they have a heart attack. As DS Harte says, they are statistically at an age where they are more likely to have that happen. If they were all killed by someone else, then whoever killed them has committed three pretty much perfect murders. But Daryl is another matter altogether. He's young, no health problems, nothing to suggest that there was anything wrong with him, which there'd have to be if he was going to have a heart attack at seventeen. Am I on the right lines, Sir?"

Blake smiled at her. "Spot on Mini."

"So, if Daryl was killed by the same person as the first three, then that means that the killer may have either got cocky, careless, or they went from murder to manslaughter."

"Wait, hang on a second," Royale boomed. He was standing in the doorway to his office watching proceedings as he often did in these kind of meetings. "You're saying you think that Daryl's death might have been an accident?"

"I think it's something we certainly need to consider, Sir," Blake replied. "Like Mini said, the first three could just about pass as perfectly natural deaths. But now, because of Daryl dying, we're now looking for what could well turn out to be a serial killer. They either have a bloody good reason why they wanted Daryl dead and don't care that we're after them or they made a huge mistake."

There was a few moments silence in the room as the information sank in. Royale stroked his bushy moustache thoughtfully. "Alright," he said slowly at last. "I can see that. Of course, without a solid cause of death, we're going to be hard pushed to know where to start looking for a killer."

"Which brings us back to that confessions booth," Blake said. "What has been happening in there to make at least three people suddenly keel over from what looks like a heart attack?"

"The only person anywhere near them at the time was Timothy Croydon," Mattison said quietly.

Gardiner shook his head. "Oh come on, the man is in his seventies. You're not seriously suggesting he's somehow masterminded the ingenious and impossible murder of three of his parishioners?"

Blake wrote Timothy Croydon's name on the

board and stared at it for a few moments. He then silently drew two rectangles side by side and stood back so that they could all see.

"Alright, so the vicar is sat in this box here." He put a small letter 'V' in one of the rectangles. "And then whoever is doing the confessing is sat in this one here." A 'C' was then scribbled into the other one. "Now, just for the sake of argument, if the vicar is our killer, having sat in this thing myself, the only way I could see that he could get to anybody sat in the other box would be through the grill that's between them." He scribbled a wiggly line between the two rectangles, then stood back again.

After a moment's pause where they all stared at the diagram on the board, Blake turned to them. "Anybody have any clue how he would have managed to make three people have a heart attack?"

"Poison dart?" Mattison suggested, a trace of doubt in his voice.

"It's not the worst idea you could have had, considering you're hung-over," Blake said dryly.

Mattison looked down at his notepad sheepishly. "Thank you, Sir."

From the back of the room, Gardiner rolled his eyes and tutted. "There weren't any marks on the bodies Mattison! A dart's going to leave some sort of pinprick at the very least. Use your brain, man."

"So, come on then, Michael," Blake said, sharply.

"Let's hear *your* ideas."

"My idea?" Gardiner replied flatly. "We're looking at three people who died from a heart attack. Young Stuarts is suspicious, I grant you that, but it's impossible and ridiculous to suggest that the first three died any other way. Sometimes, heart attacks just happen."

"You've got no imagination, that's your problem," Blake said lightly. "Mind you," he turned back to the board and sighed. Staring at the diagram he had drawn on the wall was doing nothing else but making his eyes feel more tired than they already were. "I can't say I blame you with this. That confessions booth has been there for years and years according to Croydon, it's not like you could have rigged it up in any way without anybody seeing, is it? That grill doesn't move, I checked. There aren't any doors or secret little panels. For all intents and purposes, it's just your standard confessions booth."

"So, aside from the old Reverend," Royale interjected. "Who else have we got?"

"Well, there's Jennifer Greene," Blake replied, scribbling her name on the board. "She makes absolutely no secret of the fact that she had a metaphorical axe to grind with Imelda and Patricia. The pair of them apparently made it their mission in life to make her inauguration as a priest as difficult as possible."

"Not exactly a reason to murder two people though, is it, Sir?" Patil asked after draining her coffee cup.

"No," Blake replied thoughtfully. "It's not the best way to prove yourself to God, killing two mouthy old pensioners."

"Imelda and Patricia weren't nice people, Sir," Mattison said firmly. "And they did absolutely everything together. They were like the Marley Brothers with handbags. It's not like they'd be short of enemies round this village."

"On the other hand," Gardiner said, standing up from his desk. "Nigel Proctor was probably one of the nicest blokes this village has ever known. Quiet, kept himself to himself, never had a cross word to say to anybody."

Blake stared at the board, more confused than ever. "And then, there's seventeen-year-old Daryl Stuarts."

The room fell completely silent. Blake's head was starting to throb. "I think you'd better get us another round of coffees, Matti," he said quietly.

A few hours later, an exasperated Blake concluded the meeting, partly because they had come no closer to landing on anything concrete, and also because it was nearing two in the morning, and Mattison's eyes had begun to close.

He wearily made his way down the station steps, pulling the zipper on his coat up right to the top, and taking a few well deserved sucks on his ecig. The wind, which had gotten slightly stronger as the night had dragged on was the only sound in the otherwise silent village. The change of environment did nothing to help Blake's brain from throwing around the few scant facts they had to work with in the investigation. With some effort, he pushed the confusing thoughts out of his mind, concluding that he was unlikely to come up with anything remotely helpful when he was feeling as tired as he was and began walking home.

No sooner had Blake turned the corner on the other end of the street, he heard a car coming from behind him. Blake frowned as he turned to the approaching vehicle. It was unusual for anybody to be driving around Harmschapel this time of night as the village seemed to have some unspoken law that after the stroke of twelve the streets became deserted.

The car, which Blake quickly realised was a taxi, came to a stop on the other end of the road. A few moments later, one of the back doors opened and a giggling body fell out of it and onto the pavement, laughing hysterically. Blake stopped and narrowed his eyes as he realised he recognised exactly who it was.

"Harrison!" A voice from the back of the car rang out, laughing just as hard. Blake stared as a clearly extremely drunk Harrison sat up and looked into the back of the taxi. A moment later, Callum Croydon stepped out from the other side of the car, thanked the taxi driver, and slammed his door shut, rushing round to pick up Harrison from the ground. They didn't see Blake watching, but as the taxi drove off, he realised that they were far too preoccupied with their own activities to be taking any notice as to who else might be around. As Harrison, clearly much more sexually confident drunk than he was sober, pulled Callum towards him, Blake was surprised to feel a strong growl of jealousy from deep within him as the two came to rest against a wall, kissing passionately.

Blake put his hands in his coat pockets, crossed the road, and walked past them as stealthily as he could so he didn't attract attention to himself. As he strode down the next street towards his cottage, he could feel his head quickly flooding once again with confused and equally conflicting thoughts, but this time they had absolutely nothing to do with the investigation.

CHAPTER
TEN

When Blake's alarm went off the next morning he felt like he hadn't slept at all, despite the fact he had fallen asleep as soon as his head had hit the pillow. The most vivid and bizarre dream had stalked him throughout the night. He had been sat in the confessions booth, with Harrison on the other side, demanding that Blake divulge his feelings or he would suffer the consequences.

Now, as he sat in one of the cars, with Patil driving them both to the vicarage to speak to Timothy

Croydon, Blake almost wished his alarm had left him asleep long enough to discover what those consequences were if it meant shedding fragment of light on what was happening at St Abra's church.

Blake glanced at Patil, who had been unusually quiet all morning, despite normally being the cattiest in the station. "Are you alright, Mini?"

Patil gave an unconvincing nod.

"Is this about you and Matti?"

"There's nothing going on between me and Matti, Sir," Patil replied, instantly betrayed by the look of disappointment on her face.

"Oh come on," Blake said. "You two normally get on like a house on fire. Yesterday you could hardly look at each other."

As they arrived at the vicarage, Patil sighed as she pulled the car over to the side of the road.

"We went on a date the other night," she said, pulling the keys out of the ignition. "I don't know how it happened so quickly, I think Robin was giving him shots of stuff behind the bar. He ended up getting really drunk and saying all sorts of stuff that I know he didn't mean."

"Like what?" Blake asked gently.

Patil raised her eyebrow, shooting him a knowing look.

"Oh, he didn't." Blake groaned, closing his eyes.

"Yep," Patil replied grimly.

"The 'L' word? "

Patil nodded, rubbing her eyes wearily. "And then, about ten minutes or so later, he was sick all over my shoes. Apparently, it came out of nowhere and he didn't have time to react. The way he was knocking the shots back, I could see it coming a mile off. They cost me forty quid, those shoes."

"Oh God, I've been there," chuckled Blake, a bittersweet memory of when he actually possessed a social life crossing his mind. "Except I lost my favourite shirt."

Patil gave him a small smile. "What am I supposed to do, Sir? I went to that date thinking

I wasn't all that bothered. But then, when he said that, and it meant absolutely nothing cause of how drunk he was-"

"You realised that you kind of wanted him to mean it?" Blake finished.

Patil sighed and nodded. "I've worked with Matti since I became an officer, Sir. We started a couple of weeks apart and, I dunno, I *thought* I saw him as just a little brother or something. Last night, I thought I was going to have to tell him that I didn't feel the same way. I mean, I guessed that he fancied me, but I didn't think I fancied him back."

"Talk to him." Blake smiled, grabbing his jacket from the back seat. "You know Matti. Right now he'll be cursing himself for making such a prat of himself.

Just communicate with each other."

Blake got out of the car, wondering why he hadn't started taking his own advice a long time ago, and walked towards the vicarage, knocking sharply on the door.

"Hello?" bellowed a voice from behind the house. "Is there someone there?"

"Timothy?" shouted Blake. "It's DS Harte. I was just wanting to ask you a few questions!"

"Oh, I'm in the garden!" Timothy called back. "Just come round the side, I'll let you in."

Blake and Patil wandered round the side of the house to a tall white gate round the back. As they arrived, they heard the sound of a bolt being slid across and a moment later, Timothy opened the gate and greeted them, smiling warmly.

"Hello, sorry. I was in the green house. It's a bit of a delicate time of year for my radishes, you see. Do come this way."

Blake and Patil followed the old vicar through the gate, and into the most striking garden Blake had ever seen. A multitude of different coloured tulips, roses, acers, and small potted trees and plants stood proudly around them, swaying in the breeze and filling the air with a sweet perfume.

"Wow," Blake exclaimed. "I'm impressed, Timothy. It's a shame that you have to have this hidden away at the back of the house."

"Oh, well one has one's hobbies." Timothy smiled modestly, though Blake could tell he was secretly fully aware of how good the garden looked. "I must confess, though, I am rather hoping the annual Best Kept Garden competition is mine this year. I know my floras."

"I can tell," Blake replied genuinely. "However, I'm sorry to disturb you, Timothy, but I've come about the death of Daryl Stuarts."

"Yes," Timothy sighed. "I rather thought you might have. Terrible business. Do you mind if I continue while we talk?"

"No, not at all. Did you know Daryl at all?"

"Not all that well, I'm afraid," Timothy said, carefully pruning dead leaves from some crimson coloured geraniums, rubbing any off that stuck to gardening gloves. "I didn't really come into contact with the Stuarts family at all. As far as I'm aware, they're not a religious family."

"They never went to any church services?" Patil clarified.

"Not that I ever saw," Timothy mused thoughtfully. "So, in answer to your inevitable question as to why young Daryl was found in the confessions booth, I really couldn't say. I certainly didn't take confession from him that day, and to my knowledge, neither did anybody else or, to that matter, ever have before."

Blake watched as Timothy finished pruning the geraniums and picked up his watering can. He walked across to a weedy looking plant with small white coloured flowers and gently poured the water into the soil. "On the night that Daryl died, whereabouts were you?"

"I was here," Timothy said confidently. "I went home shortly after we spoke about Imelda. I wasn't feeling too well after everything that day, and all things considered, I thought it best to get myself an early night. I had an angina attack a few weeks ago, you see. They've told me I need to take it easy. Try and avoid any stress."

"Do you know if anybody else was in the church that night?"

"Well," Timothy said, lifting the can and examining the soil beneath the weedy plant. "When I got home, after Callum had been fussing over me for a while, I ended up falling asleep on the sofa in front of the television. A few hours later, I woke up, and went upstairs to bed. I was just getting my pyjamas on when I saw Jennifer making her way towards the church. I imagine she was meeting a parishioner there, she often does. She's an excellent priest. I take it you've met her?"

"Yes, we have," Blake said.

Blake hadn't meant for his tone to betray any sort of personal feelings about Jennifer, but Timothy smiled all the same. "I'm guessing she was her normal accommodating self?" he chuckled. "Don't think too harshly of her. She's a good woman. She's just one of life's defensive types. After the battles she faced becoming a priest, you can hardly blame her."

"Battles like she had with Imelda Atkins and Patricia Jenkins you mean?" Blake asked.

"Patricia and Imelda could be very cruel, especially when they got together," answered Timothy, moving to a bed of roses nearby and pouring a generous helping of water. "All Jennifer has ever wanted to do is her duty for God. The ladies didn't see it quite that way." He lifted the watering can up and brushed one of the rose leaves with his gloved finger.

"Do you know much about why they didn't get on?" Blake asked.

"I knew enough," Timothy said crisply. "But it's not up to me what goes on with anybody behind closed doors. I'm not a judgemental person. Looking down on other people isn't what I'm here for. It's just a pity Imelda and Patricia didn't feel the same. But yes, as I say, myself and Callum were at home all evening."

Blake inwardly cursed himself as a prickle of annoyance rattled through him at the mention of Callum.

"Is your grandson about?" Patil asked. "We'll need to speak to him about his whereabouts the other night."

"I haven't seen him since yesterday." Timothy mumbled, looking slightly worried. "I tried ringing him on his mobile, but it just went straight through to his answer machine, or whatever they're called. I'm sure he's alright. He does occasionally have little disappearing acts on his nights off. The freedom of youth, I suppose."

Blake cleared his throat. "I saw Callum late last night as it happens. I think I've got a pretty good idea where he is. He certainly looked in fine health when I saw him."

"Ah," remarked the vicar. "With a gentleman, was he?"

Blake wasn't quite sure why, but he was surprised that Timothy had any notion that Callum might be gay. "Erm, yes. I hope I haven't gotten him into any trouble," he said, trying not to admit to himself that he was lying through his teeth.

"No, no, no. Not at all," Timothy said, waving a dismissive hand. "That was a conversation we had a couple of years ago. I brought Callum up from a young age, you see. He's not had the easiest of lives. I think we both thought things were finally looking up for him when he had his job at the college, but after he was laid off, something about a zero hours contract, he got a bit depressed. He seems to be in a better place now though, and as I said, it doesn't do me any good to look down on anybody. So long as he's safe and happy, he's free to see who he likes."

"He's very lucky to have you as a role model in his life." Patil smiled.

"Do you happen to know who the young man he was with was?" Timothy asked.

"Well," Blake said, putting his hands awkwardly in his pocket. He wished Callum had never been brought up at all now. "I think it was Harrison Baxter."

"Ah, Harrison." Timothy nodded. "That would make sense. Harrison was quite the talk of the village only a few months ago, as I'm sure you're aware, DS Harte. They have quite a lot in common, I think. Both without parental figures."

Timothy's voice drifted off thoughtfully, but Blake barely noticed. He felt incredibly childish, but it pained him to admit that Timothy was probably right. Harrison needed someone who understood what he had been through from an emotional perspective going forward in his life. He remembered Callum's flirtatious smile in the church a few days beforehand and conceded that it would have been easy for someone like Harrison to become attracted quite quickly.

"Was there anything else, Detective?" Timothy asked, breaking into Blake's thoughts.

"Erm, no," Blake replied, pulling himself together. "Not for the moment, Timothy. Thanks for your help."

As they walked back to the car, Blake's radio sprang into life.

"Go ahead, Matti," he said, pulling it up to his mouth.

"Just got back from talking to Nigel Proctor's family, Sir," Mattison's voice crackled through the radio. "They seemed surprised to see me, but they didn't really have anything else to tell me. As far as they knew, Nigel was really popular around the village."

Blake opened the passenger side door of the car and climbed inside. "What about his time working at the college?"

"He worked there for about thirty years," Mattison replied. "He decided to take an early retirement, but he didn't get to enjoy that much of it unfortunately."

Blake frowned. "Alright, thanks Matti." He put his radio down, and turned to Patil who had climbed into the car next to him.

"Now what, Sir?" she asked.

"You can go back to the station, Mini."

"Okay. Are you coming with me, Sir?"

Blake climbed out the car. "No, I need to speak to Callum Croydon. And I know exactly where he is."

Blake slammed the car door and walked away in the direction of Harrison's cottage.

CHAPTER
ELEVEN

Harrison's head began throbbing a few seconds before he opened his eyes. The sunlight streaming through the crack in his bedroom curtains felt like knives going into his head, so he quickly squeezed his eyelids closed again, groaning. Moments later, an arm wrapped around him and a stubbly face pressed up against the back of his neck.

"Good morning."

For a brief moment, Harrison had no idea who the voice belonged to, but then a memory of dancing like he never had before on the platform in one of the clubs in Clackton came back to him, along with the numerous shots, and vodka and cokes he had consumed. And then, as he realised that both he and the body next to him were completely naked, the recollection of exactly what he and Callum had got up to when they had fallen through the front door, pulling off each other's clothes in a drunken passionate frenzy, landed softly and pleasantly in his mind.

Harrison turned to face Callum. His hair still looked as good as it had when they had been riding the bus into Clackton, and his dashing grin still remained.

"My head hurts," Harrison moaned pathetically.

"Erm, yeah," Callum laughed. "So does mine. Worth it though, I think."

Harrison moved his head forwards and kissed him, probably far more gently than he had at any point so far into them knowing each other. "Absolutely. Thank god I'm not in work today. I don't think I could face it."

"Well," Callum said, rolling over onto his front and looking at Harrison with a mischievous glint in his eye. "I don't have to be anywhere either, not till this evening anyway."

"I don't know what kind of guy you think I am." Harrison grinned.

"A damn hot one," Callum said, pressing up against him.

"Well, I don't feel particularly hot at the minute." Harrison laughed. "I'm going to make a drink. Do you want one?"

Callum let out a small growl of frustration, but relented. "White coffee with two sugars. Don't be too long though."

Harrison leant forward and kissed him again, before getting out of bed, and pulling a t-shirt from the floor over his head. He then found a pair of scrunched up jogging bottoms under the bed and put them on as well.

Callum snorted as Harrison steadily made his way out of the room. "You won't be in those for long."

Harrison laughed. "The neighbours can see into my kitchen, I haven't got any curtains in there yet. Mrs Garret would have a heart attack."

He walked down the stairs slowly, allowing his body to acclimatise to being vertical again. As he trudged into the kitchen, and filled the kettle up he thought back over on what had been one of the best nights of his life.

Harrison had always enjoyed going out and dancing, it was just that his life over the past few years hadn't really allowed it. Daniel had never liked Harrison going out without him being able to supervise in some capacity, and as more of Harrison's old friends had left Harmschapel for university and other such pastures new, his social life had taken a significant nosedive. But although he was quite a shy and retiring person, once he had drank enough, Harrison found he didn't care about what people thought of him. Last night was the first time in a long time that he had been able to completely let his hair down, and forget about all his old problems and anxieties.

Harrison flicked the kettle on, then searched his cupboards for two clean mugs. An indignant bleat from behind him, reminded him that Betty had been shut out of his room, where she normally slept, all night.

"Oh, hello," he said gently. Her response was an obstinate glare.

While he was waiting for the kettle to boil, he pulled her large silver bowl out from under the sink, and filled it with her food, giving her extra as some way of apology for what she clearly regarded as his appalling treatment of her.

He was just filling the two cups with the water from the boiled kettle when there was a loud knock at the door.

Harrison frowned, then went into the living room and opened it. The visitor was not one he had expected.

"Morning, Harrison," Blake said, looking cheerful. "Sorry to bother you."

Harrison stared at him, surprised. "Erm, Blake.

CONFESSIONAL

Are you alright?"

"Yeah, I'm fine. Better than you look at the moment," Blake said jokingly. "Late one, was it?"

Harrison could only nod.

"Can I come in?"

Harrison stepped aside to allow Blake into the cottage, closing the door, completely bemused.

"Do you want a tea or a coffee?"

"I'm here on business, I'm afraid," Blake said grimly. "I don't mean to embarrass you, but I was walking home late last night, and I couldn't help seeing that you had a visitor."

Harrison's stomach flipped. He panicked, wondering if the neighbours had complained.

"Is Callum still here? It's him I need to speak to."

Harrison's hung-over brain had only just began to process this information when he turned to see, with some dismay, Callum standing at the foot of the stairs in just a tight pair of boxers. Blake cleared his throat. Harrison couldn't tell if he was embarrassed or annoyed.

"Callum. I was wondering if I could ask you a few questions. Have you spoken to your granddad since yesterday?"

Callum raised his eyebrows, apparently unbothered by standing in Harrison's living room in front of someone he barely knew in just his underwear.

"No, not really," he replied. "My phone ran out of

battery before I went out last night. Has something happened? Is he alright?"

"Your granddad is fine," Blake reassured him. "But I need to talk to you about – "He looked Callum up and down, then at Harrison, then back to Callum again. "Do you maybe want to put some clothes on before we go any further?"

Callum appeared nonchalant. "Do you want me to?"

"Well," Blake said lightly. "I don't want to have to nick you for indecent exposure."

Harrison wasn't quite sure from Blake's face whether he was joking or not. Neither, it seemed, was Callum, who merely shrugged again and jogged back upstairs Harrison put his hands into his pockets awkwardly. He was mortified of what Blake must have been thinking.

"Has Callum done something wrong?"

Blake's lips thinned for a moment, then he shook his head. "I just need to ask him some questions."

"Is it about what's been happening at the church?" Harrison asked. He vaguely remembered Callum mentioning to him about the deaths of some of the parishioners over the past few months.

"I can't really discuss it," Blake said bluntly. "Did you have a good birthday?"

"Well, I did most of my celebrating last night." Harrison said, smiling to himself.

Blake cleared his throat again. "Well," he said uncomfortably. "As long as you had fun."

A few moments later, Callum came back downstairs, dressed in what he had been wearing the night before.

"Do you want to go somewhere else to do this?" Blake asked him.

"Am I under arrest?" Callum asked, his eyes narrowing.

"No," Blake replied briskly. "I just have some questions to ask you."

"Well, can we do it here then?"

"We can," Blake said slowly. "But I'll need Harrison to make himself scarce while I talk to you."

Harrison stared at Blake. "Okay," he said. "I'll -I'll just go and sort Betty out."

"Thanks, Harrison," Blake said, smiling.
Glancing at Callum, who sat in an armchair with his arms crossed expectantly, looking up at Blake, Harrison walked out of the living room and back into the kitchen. Betty was still eating her breakfast. Harrison briefly debated doing some washing up to occupy himself, but when Blake started talking, he couldn't help creeping towards the ajar door to listen to what was being said.

"So," Blake began. "I'm guessing, as you haven't spoken to your granddad, that you won't be aware of what's happened."

"There hasn't been another death, has there?" Callum asked worriedly.

"I'm afraid so." Blake replied. "Does the name Daryl Stuarts mean anything to you?"

"Daryl? He's a student at the college, isn't he?"

"He was," Blake murmured. "I'm afraid he was found dead in the church two nights ago."

"No way." Callum said, sounding stunned. "Where?"

"In the confessions booth again," Blake continued. "He wasn't found till the next morning."

"By who?"

Harrison pulled the door ever so slightly open and peered into the living room. Callum, who had looked reasonably cocksure a few moments ago, was now leaning forward with his hands over his mouth looking horrified at Blake, who was sitting on the small sofa looking grave.

"By me and one of my officers," Blake replied, a slight bite in his voice. "Did you know Daryl?"

Callum shook his head, appearing dumbfounded. "No, not really. I knew the name because of being at the college, but apart from that, not a clue. How did he die?"

"We're still investigating."

"You mean that it might have been another heart attack?" Callum asked, leaning forwards.

"Possibly. How long have you been seeing

Harrison?"

Harrison' eyes widened at the sound of his name.

Callum frowned. "Why do you need to know that?"

"I only ask so I can ascertain where you were the other night, sorry." Blake smiled.

"Oh, no. I only met Harrison yesterday, actually. The other night I was at home all night with my granddad."

Blake nodded, then paused before he asked his next question. Harrison glanced down at Betty who had finished her food, and was now lying down on the floor looking up inquisitively at him.

"I was wondering if you could tell me about your time at the college?"

Callum exhaled and leant back in the chair. "I was in the science labs as a technician, or lab assistant really, if you want the official title. Nothing overly complicated, just helping to set up for classes and things like that."

"Did you enjoy it?"

"Yeah, I loved it," Callum replied. "I don't know why, I just like science I guess. It was my favourite subject at school. But, you know, when you've got a zero hours contract, it's pretty easy to be let go of when there's not enough money to go around."

"How long did you work there?" Blake asked.

"Erm, just a few months, last year."

"I only ask because I was wondering if you knew anything about Nigel Proctor?" Blake inquired. "He was a caretaker there, wasn't he?"

"Nigel? Yeah, he'd worked there for years."

"Do you know why he stopped?"

"The official story was that he decided to take early retirement. But, well you know what the gossip mill can be like. You hear things."

Blake leant forward, resting his arms on his knees. "And what did you hear?"

"Well, and I don't know how true it is," Callum said cautiously. "But the rumour was that he was sacked for inappropriate conduct with one of the students. Like I say, I'm not sure whether it's true or not, but apparently he was found in one of the store cupboards with a girl."

"Really?" Blake asked, sounding surprised. "And how old was this girl, do you know?"

"It wasn't anything *that* bad." Callum said quickly. "She was about seventeen, eighteen, I think. Her name was Claire Johnson. If it *was* true, it being with Claire wouldn't surprise me. She was a bit –loose– I think is the nicest way of putting it. She left the village soon after he stopped working at the college. Her family just upped and left with her."

"Right." Blake nodded. "And then you left the college soon afterwards and started working at the church?"

"Yeah."

"Straight away?"

"More or less," Callum said. "Granddad said that he didn't want me lying about the house all day, so he got me this verger position. He said it would at least tide me over till I found something better."

"What does a verger do? I always wondered," Blake asked him lightly.

A nudge on the back of his leg told Harrison that Betty was tired of being ignored. He leant across the kitchen, opened the back door, pushing her out gently with his foot, still listening to what was being said.

"Well, it's just being in the background," Callum said. "I give communion sometimes, you know, the wine and the wafer bread, which is disgusting by the way. But a lot of the time, I just hold the crucifix and follow Granddad around."

"I'm guessing you preferred it at the college?" Blake asked, sounding a little sympathetic. Harrison gave a small smile. It was this sort of empathy that had attracted him to Blake in the first place, and had been what had made Daniel's death and dealing with his parents that little bit easier.

"Well, Callum," Blake said. "I think it would probably be for the best if you let your granddad know you're okay. He seemed worried when I spoke to him earlier."

"I will."

A moment later, the door to the living room opened. Harrison grabbed the nearest thing he could on the counter, in an attempt to look like he had been busy with something.

"Why are you holding a pot plant?" Callum asked, raising an eyebrow.

Harrison put it back down on the counter and smiled innocently back at him. "Just tidying up."

Callum grinned as he glanced at the pile of washing up on the side. "I'm going to have to go. I'll give you a text if you're still free later?"

Harrison nodded as Callum walked towards him and pulled him forwards, kissing him deeply. After a few moments, the sound of Blake clearing his throat again from the living room brought them back down to earth.

"See you later," Harrison said.

Callum nodded, then walked back into the living room.

"Thanks Callum," he heard Blake say.

There was the sound of a furious thudding noise against the back door. Betty was angrily butting it, so Harrison opened the door to let her back in again. Instead of fussing round him like she normally did when he let her in so he praised her for whatever she had done in the garden, Betty charged straight through the kitchen and into the living room where Blake soon let out a cry of pain.

Harrison slammed the back door and ran into the living room. Betty had Blake cornered against the sofa, bleating loudly at him.

"Betty, leave him alone!" Harrison cried sharply, pulling the goat away from Blake. She bleated again, but allowed herself to be led back towards the armchair where Harrison scratched underneath her chin.

"Sorry," he said sheepishly. "She's in a mood with me because she didn't get to sleep in my room last night."

Blake glared down at the goat, and straightened himself up again.

"No," he said sharply. "Well, you were busy, weren't you?"

Harrison was surprised by the tone of his voice, and he wasn't entirely sure it was all aimed at Betty. Blake seemed aware of the harshness in his voice because he then said, more gently, "Still, it's good that you're dating again."

"Well, it wasn't really a date," Harrison mumbled awkwardly. "It just sort of happened."

"Oh, right," Blake said, his words followed by a long sustained pause. "Just - *you know*- be careful."

"Careful of what?"

Blake shrugged, looking like he was searching for the right words. "I mean, make sure that you don't get hurt again,"

Harrison stared at Blake. What exactly was he

trying to accuse Callum of? "Callum's a nice guy." He said defensively. "I wouldn't have done *that* with just anybody, you know. I'm not like that."

"No, I didn't say you were," Blake replied hastily. "I mean, I didn't think you were the type to just sleep with anyone-"

"I'm not!" Harrison exclaimed.

"No, no, no. I didn't *say* that you were," Blake backtracked, appearing mortified. "I just meant – well, I don't know what I meant really."

Harrison stared at Blake. "To be honest, I don't see why I can't go out and have a bit of fun. It's not like there's anybody else in the village, is there?"

Blake looked like he had been about to say something else, but stopped.

"No," Blake said eventually. "No, I guess not. Anyway, like I said. Sorry to bother you. Take care of yourself."

Harrison didn't know what else to add so he just said "And you."

Without another word, Blake opened the front door and walked out of the cottage. Harrison watched the door close. If he didn't know better, he could have sworn that Blake had looked quite hurt.

CHAPTER
TWELVE

"How is this my fault?"

Blake blew the smoke from his ecig at Sally-Ann's face on his computer screen with childish vindictiveness.

"Because, if you hadn't had gotten so drunk that you could barely stand, then who knows what might have happened?"

Sally rolled her eyes. "And, what about since then? That was a couple of months ago, Blake. You live in a village the size of a peanut, you can't tell me you haven't had a chance to speak to him since then."

Blake sighed and rubbed his eyes. It had been a long day that hadn't gotten him any further on shedding any light on the deaths in the church, and when he hadn't been trying to work out how four people could possibly end up dead in a small confessions booth, he had found himself picturing Callum and Harrison together.

"Sally, I'm the reason both his parents are in prison," he sighed. "I mean it's hardly the basis for a long lasting romantic relationship."

Sally flicked the cigarette she was smoking into an ashtray, rolling her eyes. Even though he was sucking relentlessly on his ecig, Blake found himself craving tobacco more than ever.

"No Blake," Sally said flatly. "His parents are the reason that his parents are in prison. Or are you that lovesick you've forgotten how a conviction for murder works? What's this Callum like, anyway?"

Blake snorted. "Young, good looking, flat stomach, and a smile that would make a nun weak at the knees. Personally, I think he's a bit of an idiot."

"He sounds hot."

"Thanks."

"Well, he does, and you can hardly blame the guy for going for someone like Harrison. He's kind, gorgeous and above all, single," Sally replied carelessly. "What are you going to do? Nick him for stealing a man you fancy?"

"Don't think I wasn't tempted when I saw him standing at the bottom of the stairs. Bold as brass, all cocky. *'Am I under arrest?'*" Blake mocked. He was fully aware of how immature he sounded, but he was too irritated to care.

"Oh, get a grip." Sally laughed. "Who knows what might happen? They might have a crazy love affair, and then realise they've got absolutely nothing in common. Then you can go in and be a shoulder to cry on."

"Perhaps," Blake said. "Except his granddad seems to think that the two of them are made for each other because of what they've both been through. I think he sees some sort of future for them."

"Oh, he's a vicar, what does he know about gays and sex?" Sally replied, lighting another cigarette. "Just play the waiting game. And, if it turns out that they are soul mates and they are destined to be together, you're just going to have get over it and move on. Go out, meet new people. You're only a bus ride from the nearest town."

Blake groaned. "I'm too old to be sniffing around gay bars looking for a good time."

"Blake, you're thirty," Sally reminded him, rolling her eyes again.

"Yes, and soon to be thirty-one. You watch, I'm going to turn into one of those old lecherous queens that stands in the corner, eyeing up all the pretty young men dancing with each other." He sighed, leaning forward in his chair, and looking at the screen miserably. "I thought I was done with all this when I met Nathan. I remember thinking when Grindr first started, '*Thank God I don't have to do any of that. While some people are out there having meaningless sex with anyone with a pulse, I'm here, in my house with my soon to be fiancé.*' Now look at me. Single, living alone, and thirty.'

"Thirty going on seventy. Have you heard yourself?" Sally asked, staring at him in disbelief. Despite his low mood, Blake laughed. This is exactly why he had got in contact with Sally. Even when he was feeling so depressed about his life, Sally was always able to bring a smile to his face, just like she had when Blake had found Nathan in bed with, what was now, his wife.

Blake was just about to change the subject to something more cheerful when his mobile started ringing. It was Sharon.

"I'm going to have to go, forensics are ringing me."

"Alright sweetie. I'll talk to you soon. Chin up – a year from now, you'll be looking back at this and laughing." Sally blew him a kiss and waved at the camera.

"Love you. Speak soon."

Blake closed the Skype call, then answered his mobile.

"Good evening, Sharon."

"Hi, Blake," Sharon said, tiredness obvious in her voice. "Sorry to ring you so late, but I thought you might like to know that I've finished examining Daryl Stuarts."

"And?" Blake asked hopefully.

"For all intents and purposes, he died from a heart attack." Sharon sighed. "His heart is in exactly the same state as Imelda Atkins."

Blake groaned and rubbed his eyes. "How? How can he have died of a heart attack? He was seventeen!"

"I can only tell you what I've found," Sharon replied.

"I'm sure you've done a completely thorough job, Sharon. It just doesn't make any sense," Blake said, thinking aloud. "I mean, give me ways in which a perfectly healthy seventeen year old boy can die from a cardiac arrest."

"Well, there's any number of internal causes. I once had to do an examination on a lad of a similar age. That was an anterior wall myocardial infarction, he had a clot on his left artery. But it is rare and more often than not, it would suggest some form of genetic thing passed down from one of his parents. Obviously, excessive drug use could be the cause, but I didn't find any traces of anything dodgy in his blood, though there was plenty of alcohol."

"Right," Blake said, hoping she was going to offer him something he could actually work with.

"But, if we're talking about how to murder someone by making them have a heart attack," Sharon continued. "There's a couple of ways. Electrocution for one, but as there were no marks on his body, no joule or flash burns, you can rule that out."

"And what else?"

"Well, there are some types of poison that can trigger respiratory failure," Sharon said thoughtfully. "Including some that wouldn't be picked up in an initial post mortem, unless we were specifically looking for them."

Blake's eyes widened. "Poisons? You mean, there's poisons that can give you a heart attack? Whatever age you are?"

"Well, yes. Technically. Obviously there's variations, but if ingested in the right manner, they can."

"Why wouldn't you see a poison straight away though?" Blake asked, leaning back in his chair confused.

"Blake, come on." Sharon replied flatly. "Do you know how many poisons there are out there? And how many substances and chemicals there are that can poison a human being? Even with the food we *can* eat, we have to cook it to within an inch of its original purpose before we can consume it safely."

"Well, can you check for them now?" Blake asked keenly, frantically sucking on his ecig.

Sharon sighed. She did sound absolutely exhausted. "Yes. I'll get it done. I'll let you know as soon as possible."

"You are a star, Sharon. I owe you. Thank you. You may have hit on something here," Blake said, standing up and strolling across his living room. For the first time in this case, it felt like there was actually something to go on.

They hung up and Blake continued his pacing round the room. If it transpired that Imelda and Daryl had been poisoned, then the case suddenly took a whole new angle, and the question wasn't how they had died in the confessions booth, but how had somebody managed to poison them, and somehow manage to make their deaths coincide with their time in the confessions booth. If that was the case though, then there could be also no doubt that the killer was somebody who worked in the church.

He sat down in his armchair, his brain whirring, thinking back over the details of all the deaths. Nigel Proctor, Patricia Jenkins and Imelda Atkins all died while in the confessions booth with Timothy Croydon listening in. The only one that still didn't make any sense was Daryl Stuarts – neither he nor his family were religious so had no reason to even be in the church, let alone in the booth. If the killer had been careful enough to make three heart attacks go by without any real cause for suspicion, then what had happened to Daryl? What could he have done that had so enraged a killer to drop all pretence and make it so obviously murder?

His thoughts were suddenly broken by the sound of raucous giggling from outside the cottage. Standing up and looking out the window, he raised an eyebrow at the sight of his landlord, Jacqueline, with a man in her doorway. He couldn't quite make out who it was, but Jacqueline certainly seemed familiar with him. She opened her door then pulled the man into her house with her, closing the door with a slam.

Blake sighed, then pulled the curtains closed. It seemed everywhere he looked, everyone around him was having a much better love life than him. Reasoning that he wasn't going to get any further with the case until Sharon got back to him again, he sat back down and pulled his mobile out of his pocket. A few minutes later, he was swiping left and right on the screen waiting for somebody to match with him. Somewhere out there was the man of his dreams and after the day he had had, Blake was determined to find him – even if it meant sitting there all night.

CHAPTER
THIRTEEN

The next morning, Blake arrived at work, ten minutes late and in a foul mood. He had spent over an hour on his phone the night before attempting to coax people into conversations, but had quickly realised that he had absolutely no idea how to start talking to somebody with the mind of being a potential love interest.

His chat history within the dating app, which he wished he had never downloaded, was full of messages to people that had not replied. While Blake had been initially quite surprised and pleased that he had managed to accumulate quite a large number of matches, it had become clear that the majority of them weren't planning on talking to anyone, leading Blake to the conclusion that they were simply trying to see how many matches they could get. He couldn't believe just how out of the loop he had become in the time he had been in a relationship. Now, there were all sorts of terms and jargon he had never heard before. At least, he had thought sardonically as he had grumpily gone to bed, he now knew what NSA stood for as he had been asked by the three different men he had actually managed to communicate with for an "NSA meet-up." Now, as he trudged into the station, Blake just felt old and out of touch with the rest of the world.

"Sir?" Darnwood called from behind the front desk as he arrived.

"Yes?" Blake snapped.

Darnwood raised her eyebrows at his tone, then nodded her head towards a middle-aged couple sat down in the reception area, looking up at him. "Mr and Mrs Stuarts here to see you, about their son?"

Blake hadn't even seen Daryl's parents as he had stormed in, and now, with a twinge of regret for sounding so unapproachable, he turned to them, with what he hoped was a more pleasant and personable sounding tone. "Good morning. I'm DS Harte."

Daryl's mother stood up. Her eyes were red and puffy and she sounded horse, her voice distant, not that Blake could blame her. "We want to know what you're doing about our son. What's happening? Have you found who did this to him yet?"

Blake indicated towards the nearest interview room. "Would you like to come in here where it's a bit more private? Would you like a drink of anything? Tea? Coffee?"

"We just want to know what's happened to our son, Daryl's father said, standing up and putting a hand on his wife's shoulder.

"I know. I promise you, I understand," Blake said gently, opening the room and ushering them inside. "Take a seat. "

They entered the small interview room. It was the smallest one of three in the station, and had very little in it beside a table and four chairs around it, with a water cooler in the corner that hadn't worked for as long as Blake had been in Harmschapel.

"I didn't catch your names?" Blake asked, sitting down opposite them.

"I'm Peter," Daryl's father said. "This is my wife, Sarah."

"It's good to meet you both. As I said, my name's DS Harte, Blake Harte. I'm the officer in charge of the investigation."

"Well, what have you come up with so far?" Sarah

asked, shrilly. "We've barely heard a thing."

Blake nodded. He would normally see to it that the families were kept as informed as possible, but the case hadn't exactly been fruitful as far as information went. "It's very early into the investigation, Sarah. We're still trying to gather enough evidence to work out what happened to Daryl."

"Do you know how he died?" Peter asked.

"I spoke to the forensic examiner late last night," Blake said. "She believes that Daryl suffered some form of cardiac arrest. Is there anything in either of your medical histories that could go some way to explaining how that happened?"

The two parents looked at each other, dumbfounded. "Neither of us have ever had any problems like that," Peter snapped. "Both my father and my grandfather lived to be in their nineties."

"And my mother is still very much alive and well!" Sarah added. "You're saying he had a heart attack? That's impossible. He was a healthy and active seventeen-year-old boy. He played football once a week. Now, stop trying to give us some sort of vague garbage and tell us. Do you think our son was murdered?"

Blake sighed. Dealing with grief stricken relatives was one of the worst aspects of his job, particularly when it involved people's children. "We're investigating every possibility, including murder. Due to the way in which Daryl's body was discovered, we're certainly treating it as suspicious."

"Of course it's suspicious!" Sarah cried, her voice breaking again. "He was found dead in a church! Is that seriously all you can tell us? We've not slept a wink since we've come back, how could we? We can't arrange a funeral. We can't do anything!"

She began sobbing into her husband's shoulder, looking wretched. Blake closed his eyes and bowed his head, and Peter pulled his wife into him, holding her tightly.

"Sarah, I know how awful this must be for you, I really do. But we are doing everything we can, I promise you that. We are not going to stop looking until we find out what happened to your son."

"It's our fault, Peter, I know it is!" Sarah wailed. "We couldn't just sort out our problems, we just didn't think how it would affect him."

"You can't blame yourself, Sarah." Blake replied gently.

"Isn't there *anything* you can tell us?" Peter asked desperately.

Blake paused, trying to think of anything he could say to ease some of their pain, but aside from the, what felt like empty, promises at this stage, he couldn't think of anything. "I know that you've probably already been asked all of this, but is there anything you can tell me about Daryl's life, his friends, his time at college that you think may be of help to us? Even the smallest details might lead us to something?"

Sarah sat up, and wiped her eyes with a decrepit tissue from her pocket. Blake pulled out a fresh packet he always kept in his coat pocket and passed them to her. She pulled one out and went to pass him the packet back. "Keep them." He said.

"He was spending a lot more time with his friends at college," Sarah said. "Me and Peter – well, we've been arguing a lot the past few months. To be honest, I thought we were probably going to be divorced by the end of the year. Daryl hated listening to us argue."

"What were the arguments about?" Blake asked.

"We'd been having some money problems," Peter jumped in, resting a hand on his wife's. "At one point, it was looking like we were going to have to re-mortgage the house. Business wasn't what it should be."

"We don't have to go into that here, Pete," Sarah said. "We're past that now."

"I know," Peter said, smiling sadly at her. "But you did say anything might help you?"

Blake nodded. "Anything you can think of."

"I had a bit of a gambling problem. That's why we suddenly found ourselves so out of pocket. It started with just a few trips to the bookies and then –*well*- you can imagine."

Blake nodded again. He had seen it many times.

"Anyway, when Sarah found out exactly how much trouble we were in financially, as you can imagine, she hit the roof. We had to all pull together as much as we could as a family and I think Daryl found that difficult. I mean, what seventeen year old really has a grasp on the importance of money?" He sighed, releasing his hand from his wife's. He looked like a man with the weight of the world on his shoulders.

"Anyway," Peter continued. "The atmosphere in the house was strained to say the least. And Daryl started staying out at night. It wasn't just me and Sarah arguing, you see."

"I mean, you know what teenagers are like," Sarah added, laughing sadly. "Leaving the lights on, the heating, the tap running. He just didn't think. With us fighting with each other, and having a go at him all the time, he probably hated being at home most of the time."

"So, he went out with his friends a lot?" Blake clarified.

"Some days we just wouldn't see him at all," Sarah said sadly. "There were weeks he'd go to college on the Monday and wouldn't come home till the Wednesday. Though we heard from our own friends that he'd be out in Clackton quite a lot. In the pubs and the bars, I mean."

Blake grimaced. The clubs and pubs in Clackton weren't known for their stringent identification policies.

"We did find quite a high amount of alcohol in Daryl's bloodstream," he said.

The parents looked at each other cautiously.

"We did wonder," ventured Sarah nervously. "Whether he'd been doing anything else."

"Drugs? I can confirm there was absolutely no trace of anything like that in him," Blake reassured her. "With it being a heart attack that would have been one of the first things they would have checked for."

Sarah breathed a sigh of relief. "Oh, thank God," she said. "We don't really know all that much about these friends of his."

Blake leaned forward and crossed his hands together. "Do the names Imelda Atkins or Patricia Jenkins mean anything to you?"

Sarah raised her eyebrows. "Oh, we know Imelda Atkins. She lived across the road from us. Absolutely horrible woman. She tried to get a petition started for us to change our Christmas lights last year. Said they were horrible and garish, didn't she Pete?"

"That's right," Peter replied, nodding. "She even managed to get a letter printed in the local paper. We totally ignored it, obviously. But yes, awful woman. Why do you ask?"

"She also died in the church, as did Patricia Jenkins."

"What, and you think they're somehow connected

to Daryl?" Sarah asked, looking horrified.

"Like I say, we're investigating all possibilities," Blake said. "Did Daryl ever mention a Nigel Proctor?"

"Nigel? Yes, he was the caretaker at the college, wasn't he?" Sarah said, rubbing her nose with one of the tissues. "Daryl quite liked him I think. We saw him around the village, nice enough man. Although, I think he got sacked, didn't he? I remember Daryl mentioning that somebody had been laid off at the college for inappropriate conduct or something. A few days later, I saw him in the post office and he happened to say that he wasn't working there anymore. I didn't want to ask, you know how it is."

"You don't happen to know what this 'inappropriate conduct' might have been?" Blake asked.

"Daryl said that the rumour round the college was that whoever it was had been caught doing things they shouldn't with one of the students," Peter put in. "I expect he was going through some sort of midlife crisis, trying to recapture his youth, or something."

Blake's mind whirred dully with the still too few established facts. Despite talking to Daryl's parents for a good few minutes, he still hadn't managed to gather much new information other than the fact that Daryl was troubled at home, and had started drinking quite heavily. He did wonder whether Daryl had been depressed, but even if he had been, he couldn't think how that could possibly connect with how he had died, or why.

"Thanks for your help, both of you," Blake said, standing up. "I promise that as soon as I find out any new information, I'll let you know as soon as I can. Are you still in regular touch with your family liaison officer?"

Sarah sighed sadly, standing up and wrapping a scarf round her neck. "Yes. Not that it particularly helps. What *will* help us is for you to find out who took our son away from us."

Blake nodded respectively, then opened the interview room door. The Stuarts' thanked him, then walked towards the exit. They were just opening the station door when they were nearly sent flying by Gardiner, who seemed to be in a great hurry.

"Sorry," he mumbled, letting them pass.

The Stuarts' glanced at him, but didn't say anything. Blake watched them leave, then turned to Gardiner.

"Sorry, I'm late," Gardiner said stiffly.

"Are you only just getting in?" Blake asked, surprised.

"I –I had a family emergency to attend to," Gardiner said, standing awkwardly, and trying with all his might not to look Blake in the eyes. "I'll just get on," he muttered.

He was just about to sidestep so that he could get past Blake when Blake stopped him, staring at

Gardiner's neck.

"Michael, what have you done to your neck?"

Gardiner froze, before pulling his collar up over the strange bruise coloured mark on the side of his neck. "Nothing, it's really nothing."

Blake raised his eyebrows in a mixture of disbelief and amusement. "Is that a love bite, Michael?"

"A what?" Gardiner said, standing up straight, attempting to look dignified.

"A love bite." Blake grinned. "A hicky. A bit of one on one time with the hoover hose."

"Don't be ridiculous," snapped Gardiner, pulling his collar up even higher. "I obviously just caught in on something."

"Something like a lady friend?" Blake asked innocently, enjoying watching Gardiner squirm.

"That is absolutely none of your business," Gardiner replied pompously.

"Well, Michael Gardiner, you dark horse," Blake said. "Get lucky did we?"

Gardiner shuffled uncomfortably, straightening his tie pointlessly. "I don't know what you're talking about."

"It's alright, don't panic. Your filthy little secret is safe with me," Blake grinned, giving him a soft punch on the arm.

Before Gardiner could furiously reply, the door to the reception desk opened. Royale was standing there, clutching a newspaper.

"Blake, I've been looking for you," Royale said, walking towards him.

"Yes, Sir – I'm sorry, I was just-"

"Have you seen this?" Royale snapped, pulling the paper open to show Blake the front page.

Blake stared at the paper. It was a copy of the Clackton times with the words '*MYSTERIOUS CHURCH DEATHS ROCK HARMSCHAPEL!*' written in bold letters across the page.

"How have the media got a hold of this?" snapped Royale. "It's got details of all the deaths! Including the fact that they all happened in that bloody confessions booth!" He opened the paper up and showed Blake the contents. "They've even done a bloody diagram with theories about how it was done!"

Blake took the paper from Royale and stared in disbelief at the diagram. The ideas they had come up with were nothing short of idiotic. Looking through them, Blake briefly decided that his favourite was the suggestion that a killer had somehow been lowered into the booth on a harness, and squeezed the life out of each of the victims.

"At least they're inventive."

Royale snatched the paper off him and opened it up again, reading aloud. "'*The strange and bizarre deaths of four residents of the sleepy village of Harmschapel have local police baffled. The Clackton*

Standard has learnt of four deaths, which are reported to be murders that seem to have taken place in impossible circumstances from inside a confessions booth at St Abra's Church in the village. Local police declined to comment on the reports, - They haven't even been in touch! - '*Local police declined to comment on the reports, but Clackton Standard understands from local sources that police are particularly interested in speaking to a female vicar at the church, who is reported to have gotten into physical altercations with both Imelda Atkins and Patricia Jenkins over claims about her sexuality making her an unsuitable person for the position of vicar in the catholic church.*"

Royale closed the paper and stared at Blake, annoyed. "And then, they have somehow got a detailed profile on each of the victims! Nothing that we don't know, but how? How has this happened?"

"Sir, I have no idea how they've found out about this, I swear," Blake said hastily.

"You might not! But a case like this, especially with the way it's been written, it's not going to be long before we end up in the middle of a media storm! Why have they singled out Jennifer Greene? '*Physical altercations*? Did you know about this?"

"Not the physical altercations part, no," Blake said quietly.

"Well then, you better go and find her. Bring her in and find out!" Royale said sharply. "Now the whole village knows about these deaths, we're going to need answers!"

Gardiner, who hadn't said a word for a while, cleared his throat while pulling his collar so that Royale didn't see anything on his neck. "I'll go start the car, shall I?"

"Yeah," Blake replied. "You better had. We need to get this case closed, as soon as possible."

CHAPTER
FOURTEEN

"**S**o, what do you think?"

Harrison stared out at the view before him. "It's incredible. I didn't think Harmschapel could even look this good."

Callum wrapped his arms around him, pointing out into the distance. "And that, over there, is Clackton. You must never go there, Simba."

Harrison laughed at *The Lion King* reference and sighed, staring out over the view.

They were standing at the top of the church tower,

looking out at the picturesque village below, but the higher view allowed them to see much further than the wall that Harrison frequented. He had happened to mention the wall to Callum, which had led him to bringing Harrison up to the top of the church tower, Callum's own place of tranquillity. They stood in silence for a few moments before Harrison sighed.

"You alright?" Callum asked, loosening his affectionate grip around him.

"Yeah." Harrison smiled. "Look over there, though."

He pointed out to a more remote area, about a mile or so away from where they were. It was a desolate looking field, with a few tiny looking buildings scattered around it.

"What's that?" Callum asked, straining his eyes to see where Harrison was pointing.

"That's where I used to live. Halfmile Farm. That's where it all went wrong, I guess."

Callum nodded, then took a grip of Harrison's hand. "Have you ever seen it from so far away before?"

"No."

"Well, if you'll allow me to be philosophical for a moment-"

"Oh, God." Harrison chucked.

"No, no, let me finish," Callum said, grinning from ear to ear. "Look at it. It's so far away, and you're above it. It's out there in a really empty looking part of the landscape. That's the past. And all of this, all the colourful and pretty looking stuff, that's your present and future. That's what I always think when I come up here. Because if you look over there, where Clackton is, and where the college is, right out there in the distance, is where my past is. And that's where your past has got to stay. All the bad parts of it at least. As far away from you as possible, so that the only time you can see it is when you're in a better place, looking at it from a better perspective. That's what I think anyway."

Harrison turned to look at him. "You're quite deep really, aren't you?"

Callum snorted with laughter. "Well, I have my moments." He let go of Harrison's hand and put his hands into his pockets. "Listen, these past few days have been amazing. I didn't think it was all going to happen so quickly. I only started talking to you because I wanted somebody to talk to about my stuff, and I got the impression you did too."

"I'll take that as a compliment, shall I?" Harrison said wryly.

Callum chuckled. "It was meant as a compliment, I promise. I was wondering if…" He paused, glancing up at Harrison, possibly to gauge his reaction.

"What?" Harrison asked.

"I was wondering if you wanted to make it, you know, a bit more *official* between us."

Harrison turned his head, surprised. "What, you mean, me and you become official?"

"Well, yeah," Callum said, looking nervous. "I'll get it if you don't. I know you've been through a lot, and that we've not known each other all that long, but I just think we've got so much in common, I really, *really* like you, and I just think that we'd be good together. What do you think?"

Harrison looked out at the village beneath them again. He didn't know why he felt surprised at the question. It had been a mind-blowing few days, and he had never met anyone like Callum before. He glanced out at Halfmile Farm in the distance again. It looked gloomy and foreboding, not helped by the series of large ominous black clouds that had started to gather on the horizon. If that was his past, it didn't look inviting or like anything he wanted to look back on. From where they were standing, Harrison could also see the police station. He realised that pining over something that was never going to happen for the rest of his life wasn't something he wanted to do either. Blake was a great guy, one of the best that Harrison had ever known, but he realised he was kidding himself if he thought anything other than friendship was ever going to happen between him and the dashing enigmatic police officer he had met the day his life changed forever. The time had come to move and look forward.

"Yeah, alright," he said simply, taking a firm grip of his new boyfriend's hand again. "Let's do it."

Callum smiled, delighted and apparently surprised. "Yeah?"

Harrison nodded, returning the grin. "Yeah."

They kissed and Harrison felt at peace and secure, more so than he had done in years.

Somebody clearing their throat behind them broke the moment. They turned to see Jennifer Greene standing behind them, looking stern.

"I thought I'd find you up here. You know you're not allowed, especially with somebody who doesn't even work here," she said sharply. "The confirmation service is in ten minutes. You're supposed to be ready by now, aren't you?"

Callum rolled his eyes. "Yes, I'm coming. I've just chosen to spend a few minutes with my new boyfriend, if that's alright with you?"

"How touching," Jennifer said briskly. "I hate to break up this romantic moment, but Father Croydon wants to know where you are, so if you would? The bishop is here and we need to be ready!"

Without waiting for a reply, she turned on her heels and disappeared through the old wooden door leading out to the church tower.

Harrison shivered. The wind was starting to blow, and in the few moments that he hadn't been looking out over the horizon, the skyline had turned even more tumultuous, with dark menacing clouds really starting to gather.

"I didn't feel the cold till she came out," he said lightly.

"She's in a foul mood. Mind you, I think I would be if I was being accused of murder, wouldn't you? Did you see the paper?" Callum asked, lowering his voice.

"Yeah. Do you really think she did it?"

"She's the only one with an axe to grind over anybody. And frankly, she's that much of a miserable cow I wouldn't put anything past her. God knows how she did it though, or what Daryl did to deserve it. I'm surprised she's showing her face in public at all. I wouldn't be." He pulled Harrison in for another brief kiss. "I've got to go. Are you staying around? It's not a long service, I promise. We can maybe go back to yours afterwards?" He raised one eyebrow, a mischievous glint in his eye.

Harrison grinned again. "How can you stand there under God's watchful eye with such sinful thoughts in your head?"

"It's a gift." Callum shrugged. "You staying?"

"Yeah. So long as I won't distract you too much?"

"You can distract me all you like," Callum said, giving Harrison that addictive smile.

Twenty minutes later, Harrison was sat at the back

of the church. He had never been a religious person, so listening to the, what he considered to be, dreary organ music, and watching all the pomp and ceremony of the confirmation service, it wasn't very hard to work out why.

As the organ came to a musical crescendo, a procession began to proceed down the aisle, with Callum leading the way, holding a tall golden crucifix. As he passed Harrison, he winked, then turned his head back forward. Behind him was Timothy Croydon, looking resplendent in a long flowing cassock that looked much younger than the man wearing it. Beside him was a younger looking man, who, judging by the red and gold mitre on his head was the bishop who Jennifer had been so keen to impress. Jennifer herself was walking slowly behind the bishop, but her head was bowed. She looked incredibly uncomfortable, and as she made her way with the procession down the aisle, Harrison could see why.

The congregation was full to bursting with people. Harrison had assumed that this was the norm for an apparently special service, but as he looked closer at the crowd in front of him, he realised that they were all whispering at one another, and throwing Jennifer outraged and furious accusing looks.

An elderly couple just in front of Harrison leant towards each other as the formation passed them. "Don't know how she's got the nerve to show her face in public."

Her husband nodded in agreement. "I didn't think she'd actually show up!"

From this, Harrison came to the conclusion that the huge audience for the service was simply to gossip and gawp. When Daniel had died, Harrison had found himself as suspect to his murder, so despite Jennifer's cold persona, he felt a huge pang of sympathy for her – he had been on the receiving end of some of the looks she was getting, and it wasn't a nice feeling. However, after everything Callum had told him about the deaths in the church, and the bad feelings between Jennifer and the two ladies that had died, Harrison was struggling to see how the murderer could be anybody else.

The organ music came to a finish and the service began. Harrison watched as Callum bowed his head nonchalantly at the bishop, and moved to the side of the altar to his seat, placing the crucifix in a holder as he did so.

The bishop stood up and in a low, drawling voice welcomed everybody to the service, commenting on how nice it was to see such a packed congregation. Harrison doubted he had any clue as to the real reason why there were so many people there.

The service continued, but throughout all the young congregates stepping up for their confirmation, the low rumble of voices amongst the congregation never faulted. As time went on, Jennifer Greene never looked up unless she was required within the service.

Once all the confirmations had been completed, a group of them gathered at the altar and kneeled to be given communion. Harrison was just watching Callum go round with the wafers and wine when the doors to the church creaked open. Harrison glanced at the door and was surprised to see Blake stroll in, followed by Gardiner. The low rumblings of whispers amongst the congregation grew louder as people in the church realised the police arrived. Harrison, along with the majority of the congregation turned to see Jennifer's response. She looked up and her face of malcontent at Blake's entrance apparently told the congregation all it needed to know.

"Look at her!" said the woman in front of Harrison, not even bothering to keep her voice down now. "If that isn't the face of a guilty woman, I don't know what is!"

Harrison leaned forwards. "You know, it *is* innocent until proven guilty."

The old couple turned back to Harrison, disgruntled and surprised. "Oh, she's a murderer! Look at her – and why else would the police be here? You mark my words."

Blake stopped at the back of the church behind Harrison and watched as the communion continued. Jennifer apparently couldn't take any more hassle from the congregation, who now were talking loudly amongst themselves, and the odd jeer had even started to ring out over the buzzing noise amongst them. She stood up, bowed briefly at the bishop, and started making her way towards the back of the church, almost knocking Callum, who was in the middle of tipping the wine goblet towards someone's mouth, forwards over the altar.

The noise from the congregation became more discernible.

"She's making a run for it!"

"She knows she's been caught!"

"I hope the papers tell us how she did it."

"Why would you run if you weren't guilty?"

Jennifer stopped as Blake, watching her carefully, began to walk down the aisle with Gardiner, looking as stern as Harrison remembered him, following closely behind. With the noise in the church now at deafening levels, Harrison glanced at Callum who looked at him with his eyebrows raised.

"Excuse me! Can we have a bit of calm please?" shouted Timothy over the noise, and looking extremely upset, glancing at the bishop who looked outraged. "Please! Ladies and gentlemen, a bit of decorum!"

Jennifer made her way round to the front of the altar and looked out at the congregation, with a pleading look in her eyes. "Please!" she cried. "It wasn't me! I didn't do anything to those people!"

"Even the papers know it was you!"

"That poor family who's lost their son!"

"You're evil!"

"What are you waiting for?" somebody shouted at Blake. "Arrest her!"

The bishop stood up furiously and muttered something into Timothy's ear. Timothy looked absolutely pale and looked like he had started to sweat. "*Ladies and gentlemen!*" he shouted. "*Please! Control yourselves! Leave her alone!*"

Blake stepped forwards and held out a hand towards Jennifer. "Jennifer, I'd like to speak to you. Would you come with me please?"

A nasty jeering cheer rumbled round the church.

"No, please! Detective Harte!" Timothy exclaimed. "I'm sure you don't –Jennifer hasn't-"

But then he stopped speaking mid-sentence. As suddenly as the noise amongst the congregation had risen, it was silenced. Harrison stood up, craning his neck with a frown to see what was happening.

"Father?" Jennifer said, turning towards him. But it didn't seem like Timothy could hear him. Suddenly, he spluttered, clutching his chest, and keeled over, landing hard on the cold marble floor beneath him. A huge collective gasp reverberated around the church.

"*Granddad!*" Callum yelled, dropping the silver goblet with a clatter and rushing to him.

Blake ran forwards. "*Out of the way!*" he shouted. He knelt by Timothy and pulled his radio up to his lips. "Ambulance required at St. Abra's church, *immediately*. Suspected heart attack, *repeat,* urgent medical assistance required at St Abra's church, over."

The radio crackled in response, but over the noise of the congregation, it was impossible to hear.

"Did you hear that?" the old woman in front of Harrison said to her husband. "Heart attack! She's done it to the vicar now!"

Harrison had had enough of the events being commentated by the gossiping old couple so he stood up to see what was happening for himself.

Blake was now kneeled by Timothy, while Callum stood over him, looking horrified and shaking. Harrison rushed over to him and gripped him tightly.

"Harrison- I can't lose him, what's *happening* to him?"

"It's going to be okay," Harrison said sharply, though looking at the old vicar, he wasn't quite sure he believed what he was saying.

"Father…" Jennifer knelt down besides Blake and gripped Timothy's hand.

"Jennifer, stand back," Blake said firmly.

But as Blake went to move Jennifer away, Timothy grabbed her hand and pulled her forwards, convulsing in pain. "*Jennifer – argh! - Jennifer…*"

The whole church went silent as Timothy pulled

Jennifer closer, only able to manage a whisper.

"Jennifer *-tell him-confess!*"

He cried out in pain again, his eyes glazing over, before his head fell backwards into Jennifer's arms. Another huge gasp echoed round the church from the horrified gathering crowd as Timothy Croydon closed his eyes.

CHAPTER
FIFTEEN

B lake's mind whirred as he and Gardiner shepherded the crowd from the church outside, and out of the way of the paramedics. As they rushed inside the church, Blake watched Harrison holding tightly onto Callum, who seemed incapable of speech, and had his head nestled into Harrison's shoulder. Maybe Timothy had been right, Blake thought glumly, when he had said that the two of them had so much in common. Harrison knew what it was like to lose people close to him and there was nobody better to deal with Callum's grief if Timothy didn't make it.

The question of whether Timothy's heart attack was deliberate or just from natural causes was the only thing on the crowd's lips. They were all ignoring Gardiner telling them all to keep right away from the church entrance, and gossiping amongst themselves. Blake could hardly blame them as this was the very thought that was going through his own mind. They had all seen him clutching his chest and keel over. He had also clearly been feeling pains in his arm, which would suggest to all intents and purposes that it had just been a tragic heart attack, but at this point in such a bizarre investigation, Blake wasn't sure what to believe.

Jennifer was sat on her own, away from the rest of the crowd, on one of the stone steps staring out into space.

"Oh, I hope he's alright."

Blake turned behind him to see who had spoken to him. Jacqueline was stood there, wearing a pink chiffon dress that didn't go with her dark crimson hair.

"He's in safe hands," Blake said, trying to usher her towards the rest of the crowd.

"That man knows my deepest and darkest secrets," Jacqueline said thoughtfully. "And he's a lovely man. I've told him about some of my little – *well* – let's call them liaisons with the odd gentleman, and he's never had a cross word to say."

"He's hardly going to judge about a few one night stands is he?" Blake said as he moved Jacqueline away from the door. "Two single people can do what they like can't they?"

Jacqueline went slightly red. "Well, not all of them have been single," she said quietly. "But I can't help it if someone's marriage isn't working. I don't have anything to be ashamed about, do I?"

Blake rolled his eyes as he led Jacqueline to the crowd.

"Hello, Michael," Jacqueline said, smiling flirtatiously at Gardiner. "I had a lovely time last night, we must do it again."

Gardiner cleared his throat awkwardly and continued pacing around the crowd.

Blake stared, stunned at the pair of them, and then at Gardiner's neck. But before he could consider the possibility that Jacqueline was the reason for his love bite, the church doors were flung open, and the next moment the paramedics were rushing Timothy's lifeless body out of the church and towards the ambulance. Blake looked up at Callum expecting him to rush towards the ambulance and demand to go with them. Instead, he just closed his eyes, moved away from Harrison, and walked back into the church.

"Callum?" Harrison called, but by that point the doors to the ambulance had already been slammed shut, and it quickly sped away with its sirens blaring.

Blake made his way towards Jennifer, who glanced up at him, looking dazed. "Shall we go Jennifer?"

"I-I need to see if Father Croydon is alright," she mumbled, appearing disorientated.

"He's on his way to the hospital and they'll do the best they can for him," Blake said, not unkindly. "But me and you really need to talk, don't you think? And I'm sure you'd like to get away from all of this lot."

He nodded his head towards the crowd, which now the dramatic events were coming to an end had begun to disperse, but accusing looks and comments were still be thrown at Jennifer as they left.

Jennifer stood up without another word and walked with Blake back to the police car.

"I hope they throw away the key!" snapped a voice from the crowd.

Gardiner stepped forwards. "Any more like that from you, and you'll be the one in a cell!" he snarled.

The congregation sidled off, still mumbling to each other, but without any more barbed comments being heckled.

"Thank you, Michael," Blake said quietly. "Don't forget to keep your neck covered."

Gardiner quickly pulled his collar up as they put Jennifer into the back of the car and closed the door. Blake exhaled as he watched the crowd walk away.

"I don't even know what to think any more,"

Blake said quietly to Gardiner.

Gardiner shook his head. "Neither do I. What did Croydon mean? What does he want her to confess to? His death?"

"I don't know," Blake said. "But whatever it is, she's going to do it by the time we're done interviewing her." He paused, then said, "Strange how Croydon's grandson didn't want to go with him in the ambulance, don't you think? He seemed upset enough when it was happening."

Gardiner shrugged. "Maybe he couldn't face it. Not like he could do a lot anyway, is it? Best to let the paramedics deal with it."

"But his granddad had an angina attack not long ago." Blake frowned. "Wouldn't you be terrified that this could be something more serious?"

"I don't know how these kids' minds work these days," Gardiner grumbled. "Maybe he wanted to pick something out of the church for his granddad. Shall we go?"

Blake conceded that was a possibility, but it still seemed strange to him.

As he opened his passenger side seat, he turned back to the church and watched as Harrison walked back inside after Callum. The way Harrison had been comforting him told him everything he needed to know about where their relationship was since yesterday. His last thought before climbing into the car was that he hoped that whatever happened between him and Callum, Harrison was treated better than he had been before.

Blake and Gardiner watched through the one way mirrored window as Jennifer sat in the interview room silently, her hands crossed and looking down with her eyes closed.

"What's she doing?" Gardiner asked quietly.

"Praying, I assume," Blake replied.

"Would an innocent woman pray?" Gardiner pointed out.

Blake paused as a thought that had been bothering him since they had been at the church all of a sudden clicked into place in his head. "Possibly. Come on."

They walked into the interview room. The sound of the door opening made Jennifer jump but she didn't say anything as Blake and Gardiner sat down in front of her.

"Do you want your solicitor present before we begin?" Blake asked her.

"I have all the representation I need," Jennifer said, glancing upwards.

"Okay," Blake said. He leant across the desk and clicked the recorder on. "Interview commencing at 16:56. Present are myself, Detective Sergeant Blake Harte, Sergeant Michael Gardiner, and Jennifer Greene."

He paused, then crossed his hands together, thinking about how to form his first question.

"Okay, Jennifer. You know why we're here."

"I told you everything I know when you interviewed me the other day," Jennifer responded calmly. "I just want to see if Father Croydon is alright."

"He's being cared for in the hospital," Blake said. "If anything changes, then we'll talk about it then. But, as you brought up the Reverend Timothy Croydon, let's talk about your relationship with him."

Jennifer mouth thinned slightly, but she didn't reply.

"How long have you known him?"

Jennifer hesitated. "A long time. I don't know how long."

"At a rough estimate?"

"I couldn't tell you."

"Try."

Jennifer didn't say anything. She just stared at Blake. It was all he needed to push forward with what he was thinking.

"You see, Jennifer, there's something bugging me about your relationship with Timothy."

"Such as?" she asked quietly.

"When we were in the church earlier, and Timothy had his heart attack, there were two people in the church, out of everybody there, who were more terrified and upset than anybody else. One of them was Callum, his grandson. Understandable, I think, don't you? For Callum to be upset? I mean after all – we're talking about his granddad. Somebody who's raised him pretty much all of his life and been there as a constant parental figure in absence of everybody else. So I could understand why he'd be so scared and emotional about this, can't you?"

Jennifer nodded. "They are very close, yes."

"But then, the other person was you. The way you gripped his hand, you were in tears. And those tears were for more than just because everybody in that church had read today's copy of the Clackton Standard, weren't they?"

"I'm very fond of Father Croydon," Jennifer said softly. "He's been a rock to me over the years."

"Though, you can't quite remember how many years that is?" Put in Gardiner.

Jennifer glared at him. "No."

Blake paused. There were a few things he wanted to get straight before he continued with that particular line of questioning.

"Let's talk about that newspaper article," he said.

"It was all lies. I'd have thought an intelligent detective would know better than to use the local rag as evidence."

"It was all lies?"

"Yes."

"Including the bit about a physical altercation between you and Imelda Atkins?"

Jennifer faulted, then shuffled uncomfortably in her seat. "That was months ago."

"Well, you told me the pair of you had only talked, you didn't say anything about any violence between you."

Again, Jennifer didn't say anything.

"What happened?" Blake pressed.

Jennifer inhaled deeply through her nose, perhaps to calm herself before answering. "She was making homophobic remarks. I think her exact words specifically about my sexuality were '*You're a disgusting creature who isn't fit to set foot in a church, never mind become a priest.*'"

Blake nodded. "That's very harsh. What did you say?"

Jennifer laughed bitterly to herself. "Nothing. I just slapped her. Hard across the face." She leant forward in her seat. "And I *enjoyed* it."

Blake returned her steady gaze calmly. "I don't imagine she liked that very much."

"She didn't."

"So, did she hit you back?"

Again, Jennifer laughed. "No, she just walked away. But she did say that I would live to regret it."

"And did you?" Blake asked.

"Well, it was after that that she co-wrote one of

her hate filled and bilious letters to the Clackton Standard about me, talking about sinful acts of homosexuality in the church as well as the fact that women should be nowhere near that alter in any other capacity but as a parishioner. They published it, amazingly. I imagine it was a slow news day. The article I wrote was in response. The difference was, I am not twisted and bitter and evil enough to mention specific names."

"Why didn't you tell me about this?" Blake asked.

"Well, because I didn't actually think it was relevant," Jennifer replied, a hint of condescension in her voice. "It happened a good few months before she died, unless you're suggesting that she developed some form of delayed and sudden post-traumatic stress to me slapping her that caused her to have a fatal heart attack?"

Again, Blake paused. He was surprised by how calm and arguably witty she was behaving, considering that he was interviewing her as a main suspect in a murder enquiry.

"So," he said, leaning forward towards her to show that she wasn't intimidating him. "Daryl Stuarts-"

"I told you, I barely knew the boy," Jennifer interrupted. "Why on earth would I want to kill him?"

"Well," Blake said. "You told me that you were at the hospital visiting a sick, friend, was it? At the time when Daryl is said to have been killed."

"Correct."

"Except I have a witness saying that you *were* at the church that night. The man you are so fond of, your '*rock*' as you put it, Timothy explicitly told me that him and Callum were both at home on the night of the murder, and that you were there because he saw you walking towards the church from his bedroom window. Now, why would he say that if it wasn't true?"

Jennifer closed her eyes and sighed. "Damn. Alright, yes. Yes, I did go to the church. But only briefly. If I'd known Father Croydon had seen me, I would have told you that from the start."

Gardiner, leaned back in his chair. "Now that you *do* know that he saw you, why were you there?"

"It's not something I'm proud of."

"But?" Blake asked.

"I was looking for some wine and wafers," Jennifer said, bowing her head and clasping her hands together.

"I'm sorry?" Blake asked. That was the last thing he had expected her to say.

Jennifer put her head in her hands and for the first time since setting foot in the interviewer, seemed emotional. "This, friend, in the hospital. She isn't quite who I said she was."

Blake narrowed his eyes. "So, who is she?"

"She's my girlfriend," Jennifer said, tears beginning to form in her eyes.

"Is this a fairly new relationship?" Blake asked. "You said that you'd recently come out of a relationship. Nina, did you say her name was?"

"The woman in hospital *is* Nina," Jennifer said quietly, looking down at the floor, a single tear running down her cheek and splashing to the floor. "We never broke up."

"So, why did you tell me that you did?"

Jennifer's voice now began to crack. "Because I am the reason she's in hospital."

"Why?" Gardiner said, looking at her with his arms crossed. "What did you do to her?"

"I didn't *do* anything to her!" snapped Jennifer.

Blake turned his head towards Gardiner, hoping his expression would signal to him that he needed to shut up. Gardiner held his hands up briefly in surrender.

Blake turned back to Jennifer. "Why *is* Nina in hospital?"

Jennifer paused. Blake put his hands into his coat pocket and pulled out a pack of tissues that he had bought earlier that day. He pushed the packet across the table, which Jennifer took and pulled open. She dabbed her eyes and sighed.

"Because," she said slowly. "I had her sectioned."

"Sectioned?" Blake repeated.

"Yes," Jennifer replied. For the first time in a few minutes, she looked straight at Blake. Her eyes had gone red and puffy. "She's schizophrenic. More specifically, with religious delusions."

Blake glanced at Gardiner. He was staring at Jennifer, utterly bemused. Blake couldn't help thinking that he was slightly out of his depth here.

"Okay," Blake said gently.

"A few months ago, February time maybe, she started turning up at the church more, during my services. I thought at first that she was just there to support me. It didn't seem strange."

Blake kept quiet as Jennifer continued, occasionally pausing to dab tears away from her eyes.

"One night, Nina said that was going to the church to light a candle. I didn't think that was unusual, her grandmother had died recently. I asked her if she wanted me to go with her and she said no, she wanted to go by herself.

"A few hours went by and I was getting worried. How long does it take to light a candle? I rang her on her mobile but she wasn't picking up, so, I went to the church to see if she was still there."

Jennifer pulled another tissue out of the packet, but instead of wiping her eyes again, just toyed with it in her fingers, looking more vulnerable than Blake had ever seen her.

"She was there on her own," Jennifer continued. "She'd lit about - I don't know how many candles - but they were all round her in a circle with her in the middle. She was talking, I didn't know who to at first, I thought she might be praying, or at the volume she was talking, I thought maybe she was on her mobile. But then I realised she was staring straight up at the crucifix that's fixed on the altar, and she was talking to God. And not just one sided, she was having a full conversation with Him."

"And, what was she saying?" Blake asked.

"She was asking Him all sorts of questions. Why had He chosen her, how could He prove to her that He was really there, and there were pauses when she was talking, like she was listening to answers. Then she…"

Jennifer started to cry again, opening up the tissue and briefly sobbing into it.

"Take your time," Blake said softly.

"Then she - she held her arms out, in the crucifix position and just wailed. And she didn't stop, she just wailed like she was possessed. I ran to her, and put my hands on her arm, but she jumped back and accused me of being a demon. It was like she was looking at me as if she'd only just met me. She started screaming at me to get back and to leave her alone."

She looked up at Blake imploringly. "Well, what else could I do? I ran out and called an ambulance. They came, they took her away, and she's been in the psyche wards ever since. That's what Imelda saw, Nina being pulled, quite literally kicking and screaming, to the ambulance. "

"And that's what Imelda and Patricia were giving you a hard time about?" Blake clarified.

"Well, I don't suppose it made that much difference in the grand scheme of things," Jennifer replied curtly, wiping her increasingly reddening eye with the tissue again.

"Do excuse me if I'm missing something here," Gardiner said at last. "But what does any of this have to do with why you were in the church on the night of Daryl Stuarts' death?"

"Because," Jennifer said with a heavy sigh. "The last time I'd gone to see her, Nina asked me to bring her communion. I didn't really see how I could refuse. I say we never broke up, but to be quite honest with you, I don't think she's ever going to forgive me for getting her put in that hospital. She hates it there. And she still has a long way to go. But she asked for it to be wine and wafer bread from St Abra's as that, she says, is the place where she first saw God."

"I don't want to sound insensitive here," Blake ventured. "But, I don't think the hospital would take too kindly to you smuggling wine in for her."

"They wouldn't, you're quite right." Jennifer sniffed. "Neither would they appreciate me essentially playing along with her delusions, but like I said, I didn't feel I could refuse. Anyway, that night I went to the church so that I could take her communion. I found the bread in the cupboard, but the wine was all gone. I don't know what happened to it, I was sure we still had plenty left after the last service. Still, I took some wafer, and just took her some wine from the house. She didn't notice the difference. I didn't want Father Croydon to know I'd been stealing from the church."

"So, does Timothy know anything about this?"

"No," Jennifer said simply. "He's harboured enough of my secrets, without having another one added to the list."

And now, they had returned to Blake's original first thoughts. The notion that had been bugging him since he had watched Jennifer holding Timothy's hand, looking so bereft.

"And, what secrets would they be?" Gardiner asked airily.

Jennifer didn't say anything. She just looked down at the floor again.

"I think," Blake said softly. "I could probably take an educated guess."

Jennifer looked up at him, her eyes sad and teary.

"Because I've heard people talking to and about Timothy Croydon," Blake continued. "And they say things like *'Vicar,'* *'Revered Croydon*, or even just simply *'Timothy.'* But you're the only one I've ever heard refer to him as *'Father Croydon.'*"

When Jennifer remained silent, Blake knew that

was he was thinking must be right.

"And the way you held his hand and just said *'Father,'*" Blake said. "You're his daughter, aren't you?"

There was a long pause, before Jennifer finally whispered, "Yes."

"Are you his only daughter?"

"Yes." Jennifer said again.

"Which would make you Callum's mother, wouldn't it?"

Gardiner stared at Jennifer in disbelief. "But how can you be -"

"Shut up, Michael," Blake interrupted.

Jennifer leant forwards slowly and put her head in her hands. "Callum has absolutely no idea. I was a bit of a young tearaway in my time. I went out, got drunk, slept with men. Not a million miles away from how Callum is now, actually," she added wryly. "The difference being, of course, that I wasn't really that attracted to them. I knew what I was, but I completely underestimated how my father would react. I didn't think being the lesbian daughter of the Catholic priest would be something he would be all too thrilled about, so I did everything I could to try to change that in myself. He was however, absolutely fine about it. Couldn't have been nicer. What he was less pleased about was the fact that one of the men I'd slept with had left me pregnant. I got in contact with the father. Jeremy. As it happened, he was an absolutely lovely man. I told him I was pregnant, and he was ready to just become a single father. Which is lucky, because abortion obviously wasn't an option."

"So, you had Callum and gave him to Jeremy?" Blake clarified.

"Yes. And for three years, that was the way it was. I carried on with my life. Then, one day, out of the blue, Jeremy got in touch. He'd been diagnosed with cancer and it was terminal. He had a matter of months to live, and because he didn't have any family around of his own who wanted to take on a three-year-old, he asked if I could make any arrangements. Dad immediately said that he'd raise him. He'd just tell Callum when he was old enough that his parents were both killed in a car crash, but I didn't want to be painted as some sort of hero. So, as far as Callum knows, he lost his father, who was a good, kind man to cancer, and his mother just ran away."

Jennifer leant back in her chair and looked up at the ceiling vacantly. "Sometimes," she murmured. "I think about just telling him the truth. Just blurting out, '*I'm your mum.*' But then I think '*what good would it do? You've already hurt enough people in your life, why make things any worse?*'"

And with that, with her story finally released to another person, Jennifer broke down in sobs. Blake was just about to put a comforting hand on her arm when there was a knock at the door. The sound seemed to quieten Jennifer who merely just wept into her tissues.

"Come in," Blake called.

Mattison poked his head round the door, looking awkwardly at Jennifer for a moment then said, "Sir, Sharon from forensics is here. She says it's urgent."

"Okay, thanks Matti," Blake said. He turned to Jennifer. "I think we can take a break here, don't you? Interview suspended at 17:14."

CHAPTER
SIXTEEN

B lake indicated that Gardiner should follow
him and walked out of the interview room.
As Gardiner closed the door behind them,
Blake leant against the wall and exhaled,
"Poor cow."

"Yes, I'm sure that's all been very difficult for her,"
Gardiner replied. "But it doesn't put her in the clear,
does it? In my mind, all that pressure and stress surely
puts her more in the frame. Capable of anything if
she's prepared to just desert her child as well as putting
her girlfriend in the hospital like that? Wouldn't you

say?"

Blake went to argue with him, but just shook his head and walked down the corridor into the meeting room where Sharon was waiting for him.

Mattison looked up as Blake entered, and listened intently to what was said.

"Hi, Blake. I thought you'd like to see what I've found in person, rather than over the phone," Sharon said, producing a file out of her handbag.

"Please tell me you have a cause of death, for the love of God," Blake pleaded.

"I have indeed," Sharon said proudly. "I can officially confirm that Daryl Stuarts and Imelda Atkins died by poisoning from hemlock."

"*Hemlock?*" repeated Blake, stunned.

"What's hemlock?" Mattison asked, frowning.

"Oh come on, Matti." Blake grinned. "You never seen an episode of *Midsomer Murders*?"

"Well, yeah," Mattison replied as Sharon pulled out a photograph from her folder. "But whenever I've seen it, it's had people being murdered by candlesticks or spanners. One woman got squashed by a big wheel of cheese?"

The sound of the phone ringing rang out from the reception desk. Mattison, who was on desk duty that day, ran out to answer it.

"Anyway," Sharon said brandishing the laminate photograph from her folder. "Allow me to educate you. This is the hemlock flower, or to give it it's official name, *Conium maculatum*."

The photograph showed a picture of a weedy looking white flower with tiny petals scattered around the top of the stalks.

"Sir," Patil walked into the room, looking at Blake intently.

"Hang on, Mini," Blake said, holding the photo of the flowers and frowning.

They looked familiar but he couldn't remember where he had seen them before.

"They're part of the carrot family, believe it or not," Sharon continued. "This particular species can be found all over Europe."

"Yeah," Patil said, peering over Blake's shoulder to look at the picture. "Including in Timothy Croydon's garden."

Blake stared open mouthed at her. "That was it! That's where I'd seen them before!"

"Anyway," Sharon said again. "Ingested, they can cause respiratory failure and produce a potentially fatal neuromuscular blockage. And the poison doesn't immediately show up on a post mortem examination, unless we're looking for it, so from a forensic perspective it can look like a simple heart attack, as it can for anybody witnessing somebody dying from it."

They stood in silence for a few moments taking in the information.

"So," Gardiner said finally. "Timothy Croydon is our man?

"Was."

They all turned to Mattison as he walked back into the room.

"What?" Blake asked.

"That was the hospital. Timothy died in the ambulance."

"More work for me then I take it?" Sharon said dryly.

Blake sighed, holding his hands up his face and rubbing his eyes. "You better go and tell her Michael."

Gardiner nodded and went to walk out the room.

"But for the love of God, be sensitive. I mean it, Michael," Blake said sharply.

"I will, I will!" Gardiner replied, affronted. "I don't know what you take me for."

He walked out with his nose in the air.

"Who's he telling?" Mattison asked.

"Jennifer Greene," replied Blake. "Turns out she's his daughter."

Patil's eyes widened. "What, you mean she's -"

"Callum's mother." Blake nodded. He rubbed his eyes again and moaned in frustration.

"Why would it have been Timothy?" he asked, turning to the whiteboard and staring at Timothy's name. "And if all the others have been poisoned, then how do we know he hasn't been too?"

"The hospital said that his heart had been dodgy for a while," Mattison said. "They even mentioned his angina attack."

"That could be a sign of this being a perfectly natural cardiac arrest then," Sharon nodded. "Especially at his age."

"And he was standing in that church watching his daughter be accused of murder," Blake murmured. "I mean, that would put some stress on him, especially if *he* was the one that's been doing it, but why? What reason could he possibly have?"

"If Jennifer Greene is his daughter," Mattison said slowly. "Then, him watching Imelda and Patricia put her through hell could have been enough?"

Blake put his head to the side in agreement. "I guess so. But why Nigel Proctor? Or Daryl Stuarts?"

"Well," Mattison said, sitting up keenly. "If the rumours about Nigel being sacked from the college are true, you know, after messing about with young students, then maybe he was punishing him for that?"

"Ah," Patil said, stepping forwards. "Except, Nigel wasn't sacked from the college."

"How do you know that?" Blake asked.

"Because, I've just come from there," Patil replied. "And I asked the head of human resources about why Nigel left. He left on his own accord."

"So all the rumours were just rubbish then?" Mattison said, looking dejected.

"Yes, and no," Patil said grimly. "Somebody *was* sacked from the college for messing around with one of the students, but it wasn't entirely consensual. Apparently, Nigel was the one who walked in and stopped it when he heard cries coming from one of the storerooms, fortunately before it got too far."

"So, do we know who the sacked member of staff was?"

"Yes," Patil said seriously. "That was what I came to tell you. It was Callum Croydon."

Blake turned his head to her, stunned. "*What?*"

Patil nodded. "Apparently, the girl chose not to press charges, which is why it was never reported to us."

Blake stared at her, agog. "But Callum's gay!"

"Not according to who I spoke to at the college, well not entirely anyway. She said that they had a few reports of him acting inappropriately towards some of the students, both male and female, but they never had any proof, not until Nigel Proctor caught him in the act."

Blake turned to Sharon. "How do you get the poison out of these flowers?"

"It's not the easiest of tasks, that's for sure. It's been a while since I studied this sort of thing, but if memory serves it involves steam distillation and some form of citric acid."

"But for somebody with a science background?"

Blake said, his heart racing.

"It wouldn't be too much of a challenge, I wouldn't have thought, no."

"And he had this growing in his granddad's garden," Patil said.

As the pieces of the puzzle slowly started to come together, Blake grabbed his coat.

"We need to get him in. *Now.*"

They all rushed out of the meeting room. On his way out, Blake opened the door to the interview room Jennifer was sat in and walked in.

"Jennifer, you're free to go. I'm so sorry about your father. He'll still be at the hospital if you want to see him."

Jennifer looked up at him, tears streaming down her cheeks. "Really? I can go?"

"Absolutely."

As Jennifer hurried past them and out of the room, Gardiner, who had been sitting at the desk opposite her, raised his eyebrows and looked at Blake quizzically.

"We need to go, come on," Blake said to him. "I'll explain on the way."

They hurried outside to the car where Patil and Mattison were waiting. The weather had taken a rapid turn for the worse, and the sky above them was dark and foreboding.

"Go to the church," Blake told Patil who was

driving. "If he's not there, we'll check the hospital."

As the car roared out the station, Blake's mind continued to whirr, putting all the information together. If they had landed on who had been behind the deaths, then he couldn't shake the feeling that Harrison was in great danger.

CHAPTER
SEVENTEEN

Harrison sat in the front row of the church seats watching Callum. Once Timothy had been taken away, Callum had said nothing. He had just walked back into the church and sat down underneath the altar, staring into space, ignoring Harrison's insistence that he should go with his granddad in the ambulance.

"Callum?" he said gently. "Don't you think we should go to the hospital?"

"I can't," Callum murmured.

"Why not? He'll be okay. They'll make him better

again," Harrison said encouragingly, standing up and coming to sit next to him.

"They won't," Callum said dully. "He's dead. I know he is. You saw him. I can't see him like that."

"Those paramedics know what they're doing," Harrison told him softly. "They'll be things they can-"

"He's *dead*, Harrison," Callum said forcefully. "You know that, and I know that."

Harrison sighed. He couldn't deny that Timothy had certainly looked beyond help once they had put him in the ambulance. Callum turned to him, a pleading look in his eyes, gripping his hand tightly.

"You're here for me, aren't you? You're not going anywhere? No matter what happens?"

For a brief moment, Harrison's mind went back to the last time he had this exact conversation with somebody. It had been with Daniel, just after Daniel's father had been killed after driving in a car, drunk. A few months after having that conversation, Harrison had found himself being beaten black and blue.

But he pushed those thoughts out of his mind. Callum wasn't like that. He was kind, caring and gentle. He wasn't anything like Daniel.

"Of course not," Harrison said firmly. "I'm not going anywhere."

He couldn't tell if Callum was reassured or not. After a few moments, he let go of Harrison's hand, and put his head in his own hands. "This is all my fault," he said quietly. Harrison wasn't sure whether he was talking to him or himself.

"Don't say that," Harrison said. "Of course it isn't your fault. How could it be?"

"No, it is." Callum raised his head up again and stood up. "It's like I'm being punished. After everything that's happened, he was the only person I had that was close to me." He turned and smiled warmly at Harrison. "Till I met you."

Harrison returned his smile, a little cautiously. "He had a heart attack, Callum. There's nothing you or anyone could have done about that. You can't blame yourself."

Callum closed his eyes and took a deep breath, before turning to the altar and looking up at the crucifix. "You don't believe in all this, do you?"

Harrison looked behind him to the crucifix. "No, you know I don't. You don't either, do you?"

"I didn't think I did," Callum said quietly. "But, I dunno. Maybe there is something in it. Or fate. Or something like that. How do we know there isn't someone looking down on us, sorting everything out and making everything fair again?"

Harrison couldn't think of anything to say to that.

After a few moments, Callum looked down at him, then said calmly, "I'm going to go upstairs to the tower again. You coming?"

Harrison glanced at the window. The rain, which

had looked like it was coming when they were standing on the church roof earlier, had started pelting down, hammering on the church windows.

"It's chucking it down," he said.

Callum gave a small smile. "It doesn't matter. You coming?"

Without waiting for an answer, he turned and started walking down the aisle, slowing for a few moments to look at the confessions booth, which was looking dark and foreboding in the light from the darkness of the clouds outside, then strode purposefully to the steps to the church tower.

Harrison sighed and followed him. "Callum, wait a minute," he called.

But Callum didn't seem to hear him. He just opened the wooden door to the tower steps and took them two at a time, with Harrison closely behind.

When they arrived at the top of the tower, the rain was even heavier than it had looked outside, and the clouds above were an angry jet-black colour.

"Callum, there's a storm," Harrison called over the sound of the rain. "Come inside, we can come back up here when it's cleared."

"We don't need to, it's perfect," Callum said, walking to the edge of one of the parapets and looking over the edge. "It sums it all up, doesn't it?"

"What does?" Harrison stared at him, confused.

"All the deaths," Callum said as a rumble of

thunder sounded above them. "All the deaths that have happened in this church."

"We don't need to talk about that now," Harrison said, walking up to him. "Let's go to the hospital and-"

"But people have died, Harrison," interrupted Callum. "That's why this is happening, because of people dying!" He turned his head to face him again, and he looked scared and vulnerable.

"They've got the person who was doing that though," Harrison said, unsure of where this was going. "Jennifer Greene, that's why she went with Blake earlier, it must have been her. All that stuff in the papers…"

"It wasn't her, Harrison!" Callum exclaimed, looking at him as if he was desperate for Harrison to understand what he was thinking, the heavy rain flattening his hair to his face. "*I* contacted the paper! *I* told them that she was responsible!"

Another rumble of thunder, louder this time, sounded from above them. The storm was getting closer.

Harrison stared at him, his eyes wide. "Why?"

Callum shook his head, then, to Harrison's horror, stood up on the edge of the parapet, looking down at the drop below.

"Callum, what are you doing? You're going to fall, come down!"

"It was me, Harrison," Callum said, his voice

barely audible above the sound of the rain smacking loudly around them. "I did it, it was me. I killed them all."

Harrison's mouth went dry. "What do you mean?" It sounded like such a stupid question, as Callum couldn't have been much clearer in what he was saying, but the words just weren't making sense.

Callum looked down at him, sadness in his eyes. He looked so afraid that Harrison couldn't believe that he was capable of what he claiming.

"I poisoned them. Imelda and Patricia, Nigel – even Daryl. Daryl was an accident though, I didn't mean it to happen. You have to believe me, I never wanted that to happen! But I had to make sure I wasn't in the spotlight for it. So I contacted the papers and told them about a fight I'd seen Jennifer and Imelda having. I couldn't think what else to do."

Harrison felt numb. The wind was starting to pick up, making the rain, which had tightened his clothes to his skin feel even colder.

"They were found in that confessions booth, Callum. They had heart attacks, you couldn't have killed them, you're not making any sense."

As a stronger gust of wind blew, Callum gripped the side of the wall to steady himself. "I poisoned them. I didn't have any choice. They were found in that confessions booth because that's where I wanted them to die. Nigel had been telling lies about me, he'd got me sacked from the college. You have to believe me when I say, I didn't want any of this to happen, Harrison! *Please* tell me you believe me."

Harrison barely registered himself shivering from the cold. "I believe you. But please, Callum, come down from up there, it's not safe!"

"Hemlock. I made my granddad grow it in his garden," Callum said, looking more reassured but still not moving. "I told him it was Queen Anne's lace – they look pretty much the same, and he didn't seem to know the difference." Callum laughed softly to himself. "He loved that garden, he thought I was just sharing his interest in horticulture, so he looked after it. I made sure he never touched it, because you can't touch hemlock."

Harrison couldn't believe what he was hearing. "You're telling me you poisoned them? How?"

Callum looked up at the sky as an even louder crash of thunder roared above them, and a fork of lightning darted across the sky over the fields in front of them.

"Once I'd gotten the poison out of the flowers, I just kept it in a small bottle. Then, I waited till communion. Both of them were always at church, every Sunday morning and evening. Nigel was first. As I was going round with the goblet with the wine in, just before I got to him, I put the poison in the wine, underneath the cloth that we carry to wipe it. And he drank it. I remember the day it happened, he had this look in his eyes, just smug and glad about the lies he'd told about me." He gripped the walls and looked down at the drop beneath him again. "And he had that look in his eyes as he was drinking the poison."

"But how did he end up in the confessions booth?" Harrison asked. Despite everything Callum was saying, he was desperately hoping that it was just the grief of Timothy's heart attack.

"Oh, that wasn't meant to happen. Not at first anyway. I thought he'd just keel over after a few minutes," Callum said, looking at Harrison as if he was searching for some sign that what he was saying was making sense, and that Harrison agreed that it had all had to happen.

"But, I dunno, it didn't kick in as quickly as I thought it would. I kept watching him. I mean, he didn't look well, but he lasted throughout the whole service. But he had booked an appointment for a confession with Granddad straight after the service. That's when it happened. I watched him when he went in, and he really looked ill. I made myself scarce before he-"

He stopped as another huge crash of thunder boomed above them and a huge sheet of lightning flashed in the sky. Once it had subsided, he stared straight ahead and continued, as if now he had started, he was finding it difficult to stop, like it was a relief to finally be able to say it to somebody.

"Then, the same with Patricia Jenkins. She did confession every two weeks. I'd worked out my timings a bit better by then, and I knew that she had an appointment with Granddad for confession straight after the service."

"But why?" Harrison asked desperately. "What had she done?"

"She reported him to the bishop!" Callum cried, looking at him outraged. "All because of this crap with Jennifer. And she kept reporting him, over and over and over again! He was seventy-four. I could see the effect it was having on his health. And after I'd done it to Nigel, I just – I just *thought* it would be easier to get her to stop. Don't get me wrong, I didn't just decide to kill her. I went to her, I spoke to her, I tried to get her to see reason and leave Granddad alone. But she was as horrible as her friend. Her and Imelda were just awful people. She told me I didn't understand what I was talking about, that I was just a stupid kid who should keep his mouth shut." He turned his head forwards again, his breath ragged. "So I shut hers for her. Once I'd got another batch of hemlock together, I timed it so that she drank it at communion when she was confessing straight after the service."

Harrison stared at him. The storm above them was getting worse, and the wind was coming in short, frightening bursts. Every time it blew, Callum wobbled precariously on the edge of the parapet.

"Callum, please come down. We can talk about all this downstairs, we're both soaked." Harrison wasn't sure what he was saying, or why he was even saying it after everything that Callum had told him.

"It doesn't *matter,* Harrison!" Callum cried, his voice cracking with emotion as another fork of lightning zigzagged through the black clouds. "None of it matters anymore! There's nothing here for me now!"

"There is!" Harrison shouted back over the roar of the wind, thinking frantically. "*I'm* here!"

Callum looked down at him, his face shiny from both the rain and the tears. "Yeah?"

"Yeah," Harrison said encouragingly. "I said I was, didn't I?"

He wasn't sure what his plan was from this point. He thought he might be able to somehow get in touch with Blake when they were both safely downstairs, but all he could think about now was getting Callum off the edge of the tower.

Callum held his hand out slowly to Harrison. Harrison took hold of it, relieved that he had managed to make him see sense. But instead of coming down, Callum stood still.

"Come up here, then."

"*What?*" Harrison exclaimed.

"I've got you, haven't I?" Callum cried frantically.

"You said you were by my side!"

"I am, but-"

"Then prove it," he said, his hand continuing to be outstretched. "Show me I've got *something* to live for, show me that you're here for me!"

Harrison stared at him for a few moments, weighing up the options in his head. Desperate to get him to come down off the ledge, he reluctantly took Callum's hand and pulled himself up to the edge of the parapet, grasping the wall on the side of him for support. The ground beneath them looked further away than it ever had. He turned, shaking from both the cold and fear. "Alright?"

Callum smiled gratefully and nodded. "Thank you. I love you."

Harrison swallowed nervously. "I love you too," he lied.

"We'll go together, yeah?" Callum said quietly.

Harrison's insides went even colder than his skin. "What do you mean?"

"You and me," Callum said enthusiastically. "This is how it was meant to be, I'm not alone now, I know that! We can go together, hand in hand!"

"No, Callum – we don't have to do this, *Come down!*"

"We do!" Callum exclaimed, taking a firm grip on Harrison's hand so he couldn't pull away. "We'll go together."

CHAPTER
EIGHTEEN

Patil sped the police car round the corner and screeched to a halt outside the church. The second the car had stopped, Blake burst out and ran towards the deserted looking building.

"The lights are all off, Sir," Patil said as she climbed out.

She was right. With the rain pouring down, the church looked gloomier than Blake had ever seen it.

"We should go in and have a look around though," Blake said. "Come on."

The four officers all started walking quickly

towards the church. Blake was just beginning to wonder if there was in fact anybody in it, when Mattison suddenly cried out behind him.

"Sir! Look up there!"

Blake looked up to where Mattison was pointing. To his horror, he saw what looked like Harrison standing on the edge of the top parapet, holding hands with Callum.

"*Harrison*!" shouted Blake.

"*Blake!*" he heard Harrison yell through the rain.

Blake quickly turned to Gardiner and Patil. "You two, call for back up, stay down here! Matti, with me."

He ran as fast as he could into the church, flinging the door open. The sound of it banging against the wall reverberated ear-splittingly around the large echoic building.

"How do we get up there?" Blake shouted.

Mattison looked quickly around. "Through there?" He pointed at an open door, inside of which looked to be a stone staircase.

Blake sprinted towards the door and began climbing the steep stone steps as fast as he could. Right now, Callum was the last thing on his mind. All he wanted to do at that moment was make sure Harrison was safe.

After what seemed like an age, Blake pushed the door to the tower open, immediately being blasted with the wind and rain. Callum and Harrison turned their heads at the sound of the door. Harrison looked absolutely terrified.

"Don't come any closer!" Callum shouted. He didn't look any less scared than Harrison, but his eyes seared with determination.

Blake caught his breath briefly as he heard Mattison catch up behind him. His eyes darted between the two men standing on the edge of the parapet and the distance between him and them.

"Come on, Callum," called Blake, trying to sound calm. "You don't need to do this. This isn't what your granddad would have wanted, you must know that."

"Callum!" pleaded Harrison. "Listen to him!"

"I never meant for things to go this far," Callum shouted to him, looking down again. "But you better tell your officers to move, or they're going to get hurt."

"They're not going anywhere, Callum," Blake replied. "And neither are me and Matti. You know my name, yes? I'm Blake, this is Matti."

"Hello," Mattison said, apparently feeling the need to wave.

"I don't care what your names are!" Callum retorted. "Leave us alone, this is the way it has to be!"

"No, it doesn't!" Blake cried. "I'm guessing this isn't just about your granddad, no? It's about Imelda and Nigel? And Patricia? And Daryl?"

"Imelda and Patricia deserved it. So did Nigel!" Callum said, gripping tighter to Harrison's hand as another gust of wind blew around them. "I didn't mean for Daryl to die."

"What happened?" Blake said, desperately trying to keep him talking. "I can help you if you tell me what happened."

"What does it matter now?" Callum shouted.

"It does matter! Of course it does." Blake began walking slowly, step by step closer towards them. "Tell me what happened to Daryl. The hemlock. He wasn't supposed to take it? Did you accidently give him it? What happened?"

"Come on, Callum," Harrison said encouragingly. "Tell him, like you were telling me. We can make this better."

"A few weeks ago, Imelda was shouting at Granddad. Just about nothing, she was just being a miserable old cow, the way she always was. She said that he'd given Patricia an awful funeral, that she deserved ten times better. I don't get how someone can have that much anger inside them, not when it isn't based on anything. At least I've got my reasons!"

"You were trying to protect your granddad? That's why you killed Imelda?" Blake said in disbelief. "She was only shouting at him, was that really a reason to kill her?"

"An hour after he'd left, he had his angina attack!" Callum exclaimed. "Work it out. Look, can you just leave us alone? This is a waste of our time."

"You've got to tell me what happened to Daryl," Blake said, slowly moving towards him. "He had a family, a mum and dad who loved him. I need to be able to explain to them why their son died, even if you didn't mean it to happen. Tell me."

"The day Imelda died, I'd been disturbed when I was trying to empty the wine away." Callum sighed, tightening his hold on Harrison's hand again. "The first two I'd gotten away with. Two old people died from a heart attack, so what? Nobody suspected a thing. But then Granddad got you involved, so I had to think. I had to get rid of any trace of the wine she'd drank. Anyway, Granddad came into the vestry just before I could pour it down the sink. He was stressing about Imelda dying and whether he'd done the right thing by telling you about it. And his chest was hurting, he said he was having pains. So I just dumped the wine goblet, along with everything else in the cupboard."

While he was still looking straight ahead, Blake gestured to Mattison to get on the other side of them. Keeping an eye on Callum, Mattison sidled round Blake and slowly made his way to the other side of the tower.

"So, then what happened?" Blake asked.

"I took Granddad home, I had to look after him," Callum said sadly. "The medication the doctor's had given him after his angina attack didn't seem to be doing anything, but he said he was alright, and he fell asleep on the sofa. I didn't want to leave him, but I had to get rid of the wine in that goblet, before anything happened to it."

"Okay, that makes sense," Blake said. "So, what, you went back to the church when your granddad was asleep?"

"It was late." Callum nodded. "I'd left in such a hurry with Granddad, I'd forgotten I'd left the vestry door unlocked. When I walked in, Daryl was in there, right in the middle of drinking the wine. I couldn't believe it. I tried to get him to spit it out, but he'd already swallowed it. I tried to make it better! I tried to fix it!"

"I know you did, Callum," Harrison said, smiling at him. Blake felt a brief surge of affection for how well he was doing.

"So, what happened after he drank it?"

They all jumped as another huge roar of thunder boomed around them. It seemed to take a long time before the sound finally faded away.

"What happened after he drank it?" Blake repeated, edging ever closer to them.

"Well, he'd drank the lot," Callum said, a tone of helplessness and regret in his voice. "There was nothing I could do. He said how unwell he was feeling and I knew what must be happening to him, so I-I just sat down on the ground next to him and talked to him. What else could I do?"

"That was the best thing you could have done, Callum. Good for you," Blake said encouragingly. "And what did he say?"

"I asked him what he was doing there and why he was drinking the wine," Callum said. "It was all I could think to ask him. He said that he'd been having a party while his parents were away. His friends had all gone home and he was depressed, and he wanted to drink more, but they wouldn't serve him at the shop because he was underage. But he really wanted a drink, so when he saw the vestry door open, he said that he thought we might have something that he could take. He said he was sorry! Everything that was happening, and *he* said he was sorry."

Blake had now arrived at the side of Harrison. They exchanged a brief look in which Blake tried to convey that it was going to be alright. "And then what?"

Callum glanced down at Blake, but didn't react to how close he was. "Then he said again how ill he felt, and that he was hurting. Then he told me how much he hated his parents for arguing all the time. It didn't feel like I was talking to a seventeen-year-old, he sounded so young and alone. I told him that everything would sort itself out, but by then his eyes had closed and he was just leaning over and moaning about how much he was in pain. I just kind of stood back and let it happen." Callum now started openly crying. "It was the worst thing I've ever done in my life. Then he died."

"And you moved him into the confessions booth?"

"It was all I could think to do." Callum sobbed. "If I could make it look like all the others, then maybe I could –well- I don't *know!* It just made more sense than leaving him there."

"I see what you're saying," Blake said, his eyes briefly darting to Mattison, who was now just as close to Callum as he was to Harrison. "But this isn't the way out," Blake continued. "And you can't take Harrison with you."

"Harrison *said* he would stick by me," Callum said resolutely. "Didn't you?"

Harrison faltered. "Erm, yeah. Yeah, course I will."

Callum seemed to notice the hesitation and looked at Harrison, hurt. "You don't want to be with me, do you?"

"I don't want to die, Callum," Harrison said, sounding braver than Blake expected he felt.

"But I've got nobody," Callum cried. "I can't be on my own!"

"You're not alone," Blake said. "I've found out who your mother is. She's here in the village, Callum. It's Jennifer. She's your mum."

Callum stared at Blake, dumbfounded as below them, the sound of sirens pierced their way through the wind, and blue lights flashed from the approaching police cars.

"What?"

"She wants to have a relationship with you. And perhaps you can, in the future," Blake said. "You have each other."

Then everything happened at once. A huge fork of lightning flashed around them, striking one of the lightning rods on the top of the church. As the huge booming roar reverberated round them, Blake grabbed Harrison's hand and pulled as hard as he could, throwing himself down on the ground. He felt somebody land on top of him, so he just gripped onto them tightly. He lay there, his eyes closed as the roar from the lightning strike slowly faded away. But the sound was soon replaced by screaming and shouting below. Blake opened his eyes cautiously, slowly raising his head to see Harrison, trembling and terrified, but alive. He pulled him in tightly and hugged him. "It's okay, Harrison, it's over. It's over. You're safe."

"*Where-Where-Where-is he?*" Harrison stammered.

Blake looked up to see Mattison lying on the ground beside him. "Matti? Are you alright?

Mattison, just as slowly, raised his head. "I thought I had him, Sir."

The shouting below them continued and Blake looked up to where Callum had been standing, and with his side aching from the force of him landing on the ground, stood up and looked down. There was chaos below them as numerous police officers ran towards the broken body on the ground, shouting to each other and the paramedics.

"I'm so sorry, Sir," Mattison said, sounding utterly devastated. "I thought I had him, but he pulled himself free."

"He let go of me," Harrison mumbled. "He let go of my hand, then just…"

Blake held onto him tighter then moved his other arm to Mattison's shoulder. "It's okay, Matti. I know you did your best."

As the rain poured around them, the officers below gathered around Callum's body, twisted and still, lying on the ground as another sheet of lightning illuminated the scene below.

TWO WEEKS
LATER

"Oh, give it a rest, you two," Blake grinned as he sat at his desk, watching Mattison and Patil making eyes at one another from their desks across the meeting room.

"Not a chance, Sir," Patil replied, standing up and walking across to Mattison, who was sat at his own desk. "It's five O'clock. I'm finished for the day and *somebody* is taking me for dinner when they finish in an hour, aren't they?" She wrapped her arms around Mattison and kissed him on the cheek.

"Yep. McDonald's do you?" Mattison grinned cheekily.

Blake chuckled as Patil pulled a face of mocked outrage and tapped him lightly on the head with her hand. "No, it won't. I'll see you later."

She leaned forward and kissed him fully on the lips, then waved goodbye to Blake, before walking happily out the room.

"Seems to be going well then," Blake said to Mattison, once Patil had left.

"Yeah," Mattison said happily. "I think we're going to make a real go of things."

"She likes you a lot, you know," Blake smiled. "Don't mess it up. No getting drunk and throwing up over her shoes again."

"I won't, I won't," Mattison said, shuddering at the memory. "No, we talked a lot after that night at the church. The way she was talking, I think she thought I'd been struck by lightning. She said it had made her realise that she didn't want to lose me."

"To be fair," Blake said, standing up and putting a folder in a filing cabinet. "I thought we'd all been struck by lightning that night. But I'm pleased for you, Matti. I really am."

He pulled his coat on from off his chair. "I'm off too. If Gardiner starts giving you hassle about leaving on time, you tell him that I've said you can go at six. Have a good time."

"Thanks, Sir." Mattison grinned.

Blake walked outside the station, just as Gardiner arrived for his evening shift.

"Michael," Blake said, pulling his ecig out of his pocket. "You're here early? I thought you were supposed to be seeing-"

"Don't even get me started with that woman," Gardiner snapped. "I'm sure Jacqueline is a lovely person, but for she's too much for me. Honestly, one night getting drunk together in a pub and suddenly she won't leave me alone."

"Well, you better tell her," Blake said. "She's persistent."

"I'm trying to divorce my wife," Gardiner said stiffly. "I haven't got the time or energy for all of Jacqueline's – well. You know."

"I do," Blake said, trying not to laugh.

"So, I'd be obliged if you would inform your landlord that I am not a piece of meat," Gardiner said pompously and walked into the station with his head held high.

Blake rolled his eyes. Trying to tell Jacqueline to back off from a man wouldn't be an easy task.

As Blake walked home, he passed the church. He stopped and glanced up at the top of the tower where he had experienced by far the most terrifying moment of his career. The sky above the tower couldn't have looked more of a contrast to that night. It was calm with gentle streaks of orange peeking out from over the top of the building as the sun began to set.

A crowd of people were starting to make their way out of the church, and as Blake watched them, he saw Jennifer Greene, dressed in a white cassock stand at the door, thanking everybody. As people sidled out, they shook her hand, and Blake noticed they were all wearing black.

Then he saw Harrison, dressed in a smart black suit with a white shirt and dark tie. He too shook Jennifer's hand, and then made his way down the path towards the front gate, where Blake stood.

"How was the funeral?" Blake asked him as he approached him.

Harrison smiled as he looked up and saw him. "Oh, you know," he shrugged. "It was nice. Jennifer wanted them both to be together. I think I was probably the only one here for Callum, but I wanted to be. I don't know why."

Blake nodded. "I understand. Do you fancy a drink?"

Harrison looked up the road and sighed. "Maybe later. There's somewhere I want to go first. Want to come?"

"Sure."

They walked in silence for a few minutes, away from the church. It wasn't an awkward silence. Harrison's stride looked confident and Blake felt that he was pleased that Blake was there with him.

After about ten minutes, in which they made the smallest of chit-chat amongst them, they arrived at the top of the hill.

"Where are we going?" Blake asked.

"Right here," Harrison said, as they came to a grey stone wall at the peak of the hill. He hauled himself onto it and stared out at the view before them. The sunset looked beautiful from this viewpoint and as Blake pulled himself onto the wall, he couldn't help but feel incredibly tranquil as he felt his feet touch the ground at the foot of the wall, next to Harrison's that were dangling just above it.

"So," Blake said, when he had settled himself. "How are you doing?"

"Oh, you know," Harrison said again, shrugging. "It's probably put my therapy back by about six months, but at least I'm not thinking about my parents anymore."

Blake nodded with a small smile but said nothing.

"Thank you by the way," Harrison murmured.

"What for?"

"For saving my life that night," Harrison said, as if this was obvious. "There was a moment where I thought I was a goner."

Blake shrugged. "Just doing my job."

Harrison turned to him, grinning slightly. "Yeah?"

"Yeah," Blake said, staring out at the fields in front

of them. "But I'd have done it anyway."

There was a few moments silence, then Harrison said, "I know how to pick 'em, don't I?"

They both looked at each other, then laughed. "Yeah," said Blake. "That's quite a talent you've got."

Harrison nodded, smiling.

A few more moments of silence followed. In front of them, a starling murmuration had begun, and as the black mass twisted and danced around in the darkening orange sky in front of them, Blake sighed. "Look, Harrison-"

"It's alright, Blake," Harrison said, watching the somersaulting birds in the distance. "I know."

Blake looked at him, surprised. "You know?"

"Yeah, I think so," Harrison replied, giving Blake a small smile. "I mean, you don't grip everybody you save the life of that tightly, do you?"

Blake felt his cheeks go red and he looked down at the ground. "Not normally, no," he mumbled.

"And, I feel the same," Harrison said, nervously. "I have done for months. But, I think I need some time to sort myself out. The way I feel now, after everything that's happened over the past year, I need to just get my head together with it all."

"You've been through a lot," Blake conceded. "More than most people go through in a lifetime."

"But, you know, I'll be alright one day." Harrison shrugged. "And then, maybe we can do that drink?"

Blake nodded. "It's a date."

He put his arm around Harrison and pulled him in. Harrison rested his head on Blake's shoulder and without another word, they watched the sun set together as it finally disappeared over the horizon.

ROBERT INNES

Blake Harte will be back soon for a third mystery soon!

Printed in Poland
by Amazon Fulfillment
Poland Sp. z o.o., Wrocław